first crush

first crush

FIRST CRUSH

ISBN-13: 978-0-373-83113-5
ISBN-10: 0-373-83113-7

www.kimanipress.com

Printed in U.S.A.

This one's for Shanna Eilers, my writing buddy.
Thanks for sharing your Washington with me.

Chapter 1

Hudson Godfrey lay wide-awake staring up at the swaying ceiling. The floor beneath him moved, which meant another boat was going by leaving a wave in its wake. He'd come all the way from Washington State to Fort Lauderdale to break up with his girlfriend, Laila Stewart. Yet four days into the trip, he still couldn't find the words. Guilt for what he was unable to do kept him up most nights.

"Why are you up?" Laila murmured, her voice heavy with sleep. She shifted onto her side, finding a more comfortable position.

"I just didn't want to miss out on another beautiful day in paradise," Hudson lied, hoping she'd go back to sleep.

Call him a coward, but how did you tell a woman who'd supported you through some of the toughest times of your life that you now wanted out? What did you say?

He'd rehearsed the words a time or two but somehow just couldn't get them to roll off his tongue. Laila was no one's fool and she'd sensed something was off between them. She'd brought up his jumpiness several times, giving him an opening, one he'd stepped away from. Telling her the truth seemed hurtful. He couldn't exactly say that his priorities lay elsewhere. She'd immediately assume there was another woman.

Laila's competition was a vineyard that Hudson and his partner, Jonathan Woods, had sunk their life savings into. It was an all-consuming business that had become a financial drain. If it weren't for their law practice they'd be bankrupt. He'd never imagined making wine could be such a demanding mistress.

Ever since meeting Laila, Hudson had been commuting back and forth from Washington State to Florida. He was feeling both the physical and financial toll. Over the past few months he'd come to the conclusion that he didn't have the time nor the funds a committed relationship required. Something would have to go. Unfortunately that something was Laila.

Hudson's mother had walked out on him and his father and sister when he was ten years old, never to be heard from again. She'd hated being married to a struggling artist and needed someone more stable, or so she'd said. Her abandonment of the family had left Hudson scarred. He'd promised himself to never get close to anyone. His brief marriage had been a debacle, ending with his wife running off with the next-door neighbor and taking most of their savings with her.

For a long time, Hudson had sworn off women in general, and then along came Laila. He'd met her on the beach when his and Jon's flight to Seattle had been canceled, leaving several passengers stranded. The airline had put them up at a hotel, and he'd decided that rather than fuss, he'd take a walk and explore Fort Lauderdale.

The object of his thoughts now stirred beneath him. Laila opened her eyes, which were golden in color and reminded him of the warm morning sunlight pouring through the window. Hudson's breath caught in his throat at the loveliness of her. Even at that hour Laila's smooth, coffee skin was unlined. The beauty of being twenty-eight years old, he supposed.

"Why are you up at this absurd hour?" she asked, wiping her eyes, the charm bracelet he'd given her jangling.

Rather than answer right off, he yawned. Hudson set his long, runner's legs on the floor that was still swaying. Laila's home was a houseboat on the New River—a different setting for a woman who was very different. She was like no one he'd ever met, and from the very beginning he'd been captivated and madly in love with her, although at times he had difficulty showing it.

"I couldn't sleep, much as I tried," he said, smothering another yawn.

Laila's arms wrapped around his waist, and his stomach contracted. Who said only women got butterflies?

"That's because you're stressed," she said in her liquid-chocolate voice. "All you think about is that winery."

"Stressed" was putting it mildly. Hudson, a practicing attorney, had a couple of tough cases coming up. He also owned a business that demanded his blood, and on top of that he had a relationship that needed more attention than he was willing to give right now. Laila would definitely have to go.

Laila's dog, Mariner, nudged him with his nose, a signal that he wanted off the boat. Anticipating that, Laila was already up, running fingers through hair that billowed out around her face, fumbling through her underwear drawer to find fresh undies and stepping into the clothing he'd eagerly peeled from her body the evening before.

She flopped onto the bed and kissed the nape of his neck.

"Be right back, baby."

After Laila left, a million thoughts roiled around in Hudson's head. He would need to have the conversation today. He still hadn't told her he would be heading back to Washington tomorrow. Jon was alone running the vineyard and handling the law practice, way too much for one man.

Hudson stood, rotating his shoulders. He glanced at his Movado watch. There was a three-hour time difference from coast to coast. It was way too early to call Jon and find out what was going on.

He headed for the shower. Ten minutes later he was still standing there, eyes closed, immersing himself in cold water, hoping it would clear his head.

"I'm joining you," Laila called, pushing open the door to the shower stall and stepping under the water. She wrapped both arms around his neck, and her full breasts grazed his chest, the nipples already hardened.

Using the soapy washcloth, Hudson slid it down her toned back and then began making circles on her buttocks. Laila began to squirm. She pressed her body against his, making seductive noises that served to turn him on. It went clear out of Hudson's mind that he was supposed to be breaking up with her.

By the time they stepped from the shower stall they were almost prunes. Well-satisfied prunes, he might add.

Mariner, Laila's dog, patiently awaited them on the kitchen floor. Hudson got the coffee going while Laila went through her cupboards taking out stuff.

"What would you like for breakfast, baby?" she asked. "I can make pancakes, eggs, bacon or we can do the healthy Northwest thing and have granola."

"I'd like *you,*" Hudson came back with, immediately wanting to bite his tongue. His admission made him feel even more guilty, especially in light of what he'd come to Fort Lauderdale to do. He did want Laila, but the timing was bad.

Laila's tawny eyes lit up. "You have me. I've got work to do, maybe later." She winked at him. "I have an anxious client who expected his copy yesterday, so I've got to tweak this sales letter and get it out. The sooner I deliver, the sooner I get paid."

"Okay, if you're going to be busy why don't we put breakfast on hold until later? I'll take a run before it gets too humid."

"I'd join you, but this is important," Laila said, pouring coffee into two mugs and handing him one.

Hudson took a couple of quick gulps and set the mug back on the counter.

"See you in an hour, babe."

Laila's attention was already on her computer monitor. She tore her eyes away to blow him a kiss.

"Have a good run. Take Mariner with you if you want."

"Sure."

Hudson whistled for the dog, who scampered to his feet, preceding him out of the door.

An hour later Hudson returned, bringing a tired Mariner with him. The dog sauntered up the gangway and into his houseboat home, heading immediately for his water dish.

"Jon wants you to call him," Laila shouted from a cubbyhole she'd converted into an office.

"Jon phoned at this hour?"

"Mmm-hmm. He said it was important."

Hudson retrieved his cell phone, stepped out onto the deck and climbed several winding stairs leading to the rooftop garden. He'd always thought the garden was a wonderful refuge with its huge pots of pink and red geraniums and trailing ferns. It was a colorful place to be to watch the boats go by.

Hudson glanced at his watch. It wasn't quite six o'clock in Woodinville, but if Jon was calling, he had to assume it was urgent. He punched in his partner's number.

"Jon," Hudson said the moment the connection was made. "How come you're up at this ungodly hour?"

"How soon can you get back?" Jon countered, his toned controlled and even. It was the same tone he had when a witness pissed him off and he was barely containing his temper.

"Why?" Hudson dreaded hearing the answer.

"There's some kind of labor issue going on—a staged sick out. I'm sinking, man, I need your help."

Jon was perfectly competent and resourceful, as well. If he was asking Hudson to cut his visit short, it meant he was at his wits' end.

Rather than continue to grill him, Hudson said, "I'll be on the next plane."

The conversation with Laila would have to be put on hold until another time. He'd been dreading it, anyway.

Chapter 2

Laila's Blog
Thursday, January 10

Hey, it's me, Laila. It's wintertime in Fort Lauderdale and all the snowbirds come south. They clog up the highways and waterways, flock the grocery stores and take over all the good restaurants. The minute they move into their condos, they start complaining about the slow service down South. Yet every winter they come back. Go figure. But that's people for you.

Sun, fun and an easier life is what attracts them,

I suppose. And that's what makes where I live with Mariner, my French Bordeaux, a sanctuary, because it's far away from the crowd.

Mariner is actually a mastiff and so ugly he's cute. Only I know he's an oversize sweetie pie and gentle as they come. He keeps me company and serves as my built-in security alarm sometimes, too. That dog wouldn't hurt a fly but he sure as heck can scare you to death.

Copy Right, *the houseboat where I live, is moored on the New River, far enough away from the major tourist attractions so I can enjoy my privacy. People think I'm a loner and antisocial, at that. I've had my fill of sweet but confused seniors with sunblock on their noses. As for the wild spring-break crowd, that's an entirely different story.*

In the five years I've owned Copy Right *I've had little or no trouble sleeping. Others pop pills but I crash the moment my head hits the pillow. I love the smell of salt and there's nothing more seductive than the lull of waves to put an end to insomnia.*

In case you haven't guessed, copywriting is what I do for a living. What that means is I write persuasive sales letters for a living; the kind advertising a product or service. Mine is a freelance business and can be quite lucrative when people pay you on time. It's a perfect fit for anyone addicted to cubicles or hating a boss breathing down her neck.

Sucking up or playing politics has never been my thing. I like picking up my check from a mailbox and not having to kowtow to a boss to stay employed.

BRB (Be Right Back), Bob, the mail carrier's coming down the dock. If I don't get to him first, the guy in the neighboring boat will steal my copy of Neptune. *I'm hoping for mail from Hudson. It's been miserable since he left. One whole week without a word and we have an anniversary coming up.*

More about Hudson later.

"Hey, Laila, you've got mail," Bob announced, brandishing a batch of letters and magazines secured by a rubber band.

Laila and her dog, Mariner, met Bob halfway down the sidewalk. She accepted the wad he thrust at her.

"Thanks. Tell me there's a check in here somewhere and it's not all junk mail."

"I hear you, girl."

She was hoping for a card from Hudson, as well. Flowers would be especially nice since they were celebrating their one-year anniversary. Hopefully, Brock, the guy she was doing a house swap with, had sent her his key, as well.

Bob, more than a tad overweight, eventually waddled away, satchel over his shoulder. He headed for the neighboring boat and the anxious occupant on deck.

Gulping the salty air, Laila gazed up at an incredibly blue sky. She would miss these picture-perfect South Florida days when she headed for Washington State. Mariner nuzzled her ankles attempting to move her along. Upon occasion he sniffed the lush foliage and lifted his leg to mark his territory.

More and more Laila felt that something was missing from her life. She couldn't quite put her finger on it. What she did know was that she needed something different. Romance and adventure maybe, or maybe she was simply at a point where she needed to move her and Hudson's relationship to another level.

Pulling the bill of a baseball cap low on her brow, she tucked her naturally curly hair under the cap. A gentle breeze ruffled the leaves of the trees around her, and the sun kissed her bare arms, making her skin an even deeper shade of bronze. The greenish-blue water of the river below didn't have a single ripple.

Laila sipped on bottled water while carrying her mail in the other hand. She called to Mariner and together they crossed the street, heading for the park, a favorite hangout. During the weekday few people were around and she liked working on her laptop there. Quite often she'd set up shop on one of the picnic tables and work on a copywriting project. There was something about being close to nature that couldn't be beat.

She was forever grateful that going to work did not mean getting dressed up in confining pantyhose and an uncomfortable suit. Going to work simply meant booting up her computer and focusing on writing dynamic copy that grabbed your attention. It did not mean spraying her short natural hair into a helmet, nor did it require her biting her tongue and flashing phony smiles at her coworkers and superiors.

She was one lucky woman. Not many twenty-eight-year-olds worked for themselves, or had the freedom to change their locale and jumpstart their energy.

Laila plopped onto the grass, bronze legs crossed Native American–style. She was looking forward to enjoying the therapeutic qualities of a mindless activity like sorting the mail. She began stacking letters and bills into orderly piles. Some she would definitely have to scrutinize more carefully later.

After pocketing the check from a client, she scanned the postcard from Jimi, a former coworker vacationing in Kenya. Jimi's antics while on safari brought a smile to her lips. Soon she'd be sending postcards, too, except hers would be from the Pacific Northwest.

Laila tamped down on her disappointment when she realized there was no card from Hudson. Not even an acknowledgment that they were a couple. She hadn't heard from him since he'd cut short his trip prematurely. That was over one week ago. She'd called, but either he wasn't getting her messages or was choosing not to respond. She was beginning to feel unappreciated and neglected.

Brock Lawrence, however, had made good on his promise. He'd sent the key to his cottage. *Neptune,* the magazine she'd found his ad in, had gotten the ball rolling.

Laila had been sitting in exactly this spot reading the classifieds when she'd spotted the ad for a house swap. She'd thought it might just be her ticket out, and she'd read the ad out loud.

"'Mature single male residing in the Pacific Northwest looking to swap homes in a sunny locale. If interested, please contact Brock Lawrence at 425-555-3323.'"

Even though she'd continued reading, she'd kept coming back to the ad. A house swap would provide the change of scenery she so badly needed without the added expense of rent. Since Brock's house was in Washington State, it would be close to Hudson and so make him more accessible. Laila had hoped that by moving closer to Hudson their relationship would shift to another level.

There were folks who thought she was crazy having a stranger in her home. She wasn't that worried about the houseboat because she didn't own anything of real value. The houseboat, though tastefully decorated, had limited space.

Brock, a yacht broker, had liked the idea of Fort Lauderdale. He'd told her a little about Langley, the town on Whidbey Island in Washington where he lived, and about his cottage.

Although initially he'd had reservations about a houseboat, Brock had come around. Laila had convinced him that living on the water might actually help him network.

Following that conversation, Brock had e-mailed her a rather nice picture of his cottage with its awesome view of the sound. In turn she'd sent him pictures of *Copy Right.*

The idea of a swap planted firmly in her head, she'd sat at the small kitchen table for hours, laptop in front of her, finding out about Langley. And now Langley would be a reality.

"Good morning," a male voice said, breaking into Laila's reverie. Instinctively she held out her hand for the cup of coffee that her neighbor would place in it. "Anything worth reading?" Kent MacDowell asked.

"That depends."

Kent resided in a spacious, teak sailboat a stone's throw from hers. They had an unspoken agreement that whoever ventured off the dock first would bring the other one back coffee.

Laila took a tentative sip of the steaming brew. "How did you know where to find me?"

"Come on, now." He slid down to join her. "The park's one of your favorite retreats. Besides, Mariner is hard to miss. He's not exactly a lapdog."

Laila chuckled and pushed the baseball cap farther back on her head. Kent had made a fortune in the stock market when there was a fortune to be made. He'd retired in his early forties. A confirmed bachelor, he'd bought the teak sailboat and spent his winters in Florida and summers sailing the Bahamas and Caribbean.

He rested his chin on her shoulder, reading the magazine along with her, occasionally commenting or making a wry face.

"You don't look very happy. Anything Uncle Kent can help with?"

Despite the temptation to unload, Laila shook her head.

"Nah. I'm just having an off morning."

"You seem to be having more of those lately. A pretty woman like you with that booty-licious butt should be fighting off men, not hankering over some guy out West who's left you withering on the vine." He chuckled at his own joke.

Laila did not find him funny and told him so. She hadn't told him about her decision to leave Fort Lauderdale yet. She knew full well what he would say. "Don't waste your energy on a man not willing to make you his number-one priority."

Laila's copywriter's eye continued to dissect the

various headlines and leads, determining which were awful and which exceptional. At one time she'd considered specializing in writing maritime copy. She'd even done work for a couple of local yacht brokers. There were more people looking to swap homes, but none of the properties seemed as inviting as Brock's.

"Next," Kent said, flipping the page.

"Man, you're pushy."

Kent's finger stabbed one ad. "Why even bother reading this? I don't trust anyone enough to move them into my place, and I sure as heck would have reservations about moving into theirs. What if they left a mortgage unpaid and were about to be evicted?"

He'd given her an opening.

"Actually, I've decided to house swap."

"Have you lost your mind?"

"I think it's a cool idea. You'd do a background check before you came to any agreement. And you'd ask for references."

Kent stood, dusting the residue of grass and soil from his knees and shorts. "I repeat. You're losing it."

Laila shot up, joining him.

"Mariner," she called, whistling softly at the animal who quickly bounded over. She petted the top of the dog's head, rewarding him with one of the dog biscuits she kept in the pocket of her cutoffs. "I just need a change."

Kent was smart enough to remain silent for most of the short walk.

"Don't do anything you'll regret," he admonished, heading off in the direction of his sailboat.

For the rest of the afternoon Laila worked on copy for a client, stopping briefly to have lunch. She looked around, already missing her beautiful gray houseboat with its water view from every room. She especially loved the rooftop garden and its profusion of tropical flowers and vines. Often she'd sit watching the sunset, sipping wine and contemplating her stress-free life. While it was hard to leave, she needed to. She was beginning to get stagnant. Not a good thing for a creative type.

She'd always been something of a free spirit. When she'd first made the move from corporate copywriter to struggling freelance writer, the houseboat was the only thing she could afford. It was far cheaper than renting an apartment, and the lease with option to buy was an added incentive. The owner, a middle-aged divorcee, had met the man of her dreams, and the rooftop garden had closed the deal. Five years later Laila had paid off her loan and now she owned the boat outright.

Life had been perfect, or so she'd thought until she'd met Hudson on the beach. He and Jon had been stranded by their airline and, frustrated, he'd gone for a walk.

Hudson had one of those tightly wound type-A

personalities; a total contrast from her laid-back outlook. She'd thought him smart and savvy, and she'd liked his partner, Jonathan Woods. They were the only two African-American vintners she'd even heard of, and she'd been impressed.

In the year or so that they'd dated, Hudson was the one who made the trips to Fort Lauderdale. He'd never once invited her to visit him at the winery in Woodinville. He was always busy. Now she'd get to see exactly how busy he was.

She decided to try calling Hudson at the winery this time. If something had happened to him she'd never forgive herself.

Laila punched in his programmed number. She would not say a word about house swapping. No way would she want Hudson thinking that he was her incentive for making such a bold move, nor did she want him assuming she was heading out West to spy on him.

The phone rang for an interminable time. Jonathan, Hudson's partner, finally answered. He was all business and to the point.

"Jon Hudson Cellars."

"Jonathan, it's Laila."

Was it her imagination or was there a too-long pause before he bounded back?

"Hey, good-looking. How's the copywriting business? Your ears must be ringing. I was just telling Hudson earlier that I loved the mailer you did introducing the vineyard. It got us noticed. We received a record number of inquiries. Keep your fingers crossed they translate into orders. We should do another soon and update our Web site copy at the same time. It's not doing it for me."

"Whatever you need. I never say no to work, or getting paid. Besides, I'm under contract to Jon Hudson, anyway," Laila quipped enthusiastically. "Is Hudson there?"

"No, but I can tell him you called. I know he misses your pretty face."

Right! Then why hadn't Hudson initiated the call? Jonathan wasn't above covering for his partner. Possibly another woman had entered the picture and Hudson was hoping she'd quietly disappear.

Laila had entered the relationship with few expectations, knowing that long-distance involvements were oftentimes tough. She'd enjoyed having her space because she, too, had been busy building a business. Having a boyfriend constantly underfoot would only have made her less productive. She frequently worked through the night, and most men weren't going to be happy with that.

The uncertainty of not knowing where she stood was killing her now. She'd call Hudson's cell again and see what was going on.

Laila hated feeling insecure. She'd never been a suspicious person. But no call and no anniversary card didn't bode well. Maybe it really was time to move on.

Another voice in the back of her mind reminded her of the sweet times she and Hudson had spent together. He'd been there for her every time self-doubt crept in. Although not physically present, he'd provided a willing ear, reassuring her that she had done the right thing by striking out on her own. He'd boosted her confidence.

Hudson had loudly applauded her successes. The tangible proof of his encouragement circled her wrist, and he'd made sure to add one charm after another to the thick gold bracelet commemorating another lucrative deal or life passage. Still, no piece of gold could ever make up for his absences.

Jonathan had been the one to actually hire her to write copy, but Hudson had been the person who'd won her heart. She'd found his ambition and drive even more attractive than his chiseled features and light brown eyes.

And she'd believed him when he told her that he was building a future for them. He'd said that even though Jon Hudson Cellars was a top priority right now, things would change once the business was on firm ground. He'd sounded convincing when he said he was in it for the long haul.

Laila had bought into his promises, hoping for stability, even needing it, especially given the way she'd grown up. She'd also entered into an agreement with the winery that could be quite lucrative and would pay her royalties if the business succeeded. She had it all planned out: a good portion of the money would go toward a scholarship so that a deserving woman could get a head start. Given all that, she would be foolish to let her emotions get in the way.

Had Hudson changed his mind about her? Had someone else helped change his mind?

She'd find out if it killed her.

Chapter 3

At times Hudson Godfrey felt he was way over his head. Today was one of those days. He was on his way back from the bank where he'd had yet another conversation with a loan officer. He'd gone to explore several options, and had come to the conclusion that the only way out of the hole was borrowing more money.

Jon Hudson Cellars, the winery and vineyard he owned with his partner, had such possibilities. Making these possibilities reality would cost money, money he did not have.

He and Jon were putting in the hours. They'd done the research, but a string of bad luck had set them behind. Now spring and summer were on the horizon and soon their first wines would officially be released. Another vintner had suggested that building a tasting room was another way to ensure revenue. But constructing such a room would require an outlay of cash, and he'd have to hire additional staff to man it.

Money worries were not something Hudson needed right now. Not when he had several difficult cases on the burner. Those cases required his concentration. The legal fees from his clients were keeping Jon Hudson afloat.

As Hudson maneuvered his red Infiniti sports car onto the highway, his cell phone rang. He glanced down briefly to look at the number. Jonathan Woods, his partner, was on the phone.

"Hey, Jon, what's up?"

"How did it go?" Jon asked. "Did we get the usual response that we're already overextended?"

"Surprisingly not. This banker has vision. I'm actually feeling very positive about the conversation. After reviewing our business plan he was impressed. I'll fill you in when I get back, which should be in exactly fifteen minutes."

"Laila called," Jon informed him as he was about to hang up.

Laila. He was putting off the inevitable, delaying returning her calls.

"I'll call her later," Hudson said, disconnecting.

He'd been putting off having the conversation with Laila. He'd been too busy stressing over the business's money situation. Right now the winery and his clients had to be his main focus.

At times Hudson wondered what possessed him to get into viticulture. He was a practicing attorney with the ability to make six figures, and here he was struggling to keep a vineyard going.

He and Jonathan Woods had met in law school at the University of Washington. There were few African-Americans in their class and they'd immediately bonded. Both were young, hungry, ambitious and determined to get ahead. After graduating and putting in time at demanding corporations, working easily eighty-hour weeks, both had become disillusioned with the rat race.

They shared the same dream of leaving a legacy behind. Over a couple of beers one night they'd talked about starting a winery. After doing research and inquiring into loans, they'd pooled their resources and bought ten acres of land in Woodinville, Washington. And they'd been smart enough to form a law partnership, which at this point was what paid the bills.

Jon and Hudson had both watched their families struggle to put food on the table. Having that experience made them want to provide a better life for the families they planned on having. What neither had realized was just how much work and capital went into starting a winery.

Hudson's phone rang again. Without looking at the dial, he picked up.

"Hudson, are you okay?"

Laila's voice made the familiar pangs of guilt surface. He'd kept pushing off the unpleasant task of officially breaking up. After much agonizing, he'd come to the difficult conclusion that he didn't have the time or financial means to engage in a relationship. It wasn't fair to pull a woman he cared for into a mess.

"Hey, girl, good to hear from you," Hudson said, forcing enthusiasm into his voice. "I've been really busy but I'm fine." He gave her the standard answer most men resorted to when an honest response could create conflict.

"Too busy to acknowledge our anniversary?" she gently chastised.

Anniversary? Had it been one year already? It had gone clear out of his head. He wanted to ask if it had already passed but didn't think that was wise.

"I'm sorry." Hudson made a mental note to send Laila roses. Although that might be misleading, he did owe her at least that. "I'm on a tough case and on top of that we're in the middle of our first wine production. Jon and I need to have at least five hundred cases ready to market."

"You must be excited," Laila said, sounding far more enthusiastic than him. "You've worked so long and so hard. You must have a grand opening, a really big bash to celebrate. I want to attend and toast your success."

Laila had always been his biggest cheerleader. The way she accepted his infrequent visits to Fort Lauderdale, and his explanation for not being completely available, made him feel even worse.

"We should throw a party," he answered. "I'll let you know what we plan."

There was a lengthy pause on the other end. Laila was either disappointed he hadn't come right out and invited her, or picking up that he was already distancing himself.

"When will we see each other again?" she asked.

Guilt washed over him in waves. Maybe he should cut things off right now, though doing it over the phone seemed unnecessarily cruel. She technically was his employee. She'd also supported him and accepted him for who he was. He cared for her but he couldn't afford to commit his emotions at this point. He needed to stay focused.

A young, vibrant, successful woman needed an established man, not some thirty-five-year-old struggling to hold on to a business. In a couple of years the winery would break even, and if she was still free, then perhaps they could take their relationship to another level.

"We'll talk about this another time," Hudson said, chickening out. "I'll call you later."

Hudson's mind was still on Laila when he eased

the Infiniti through the huge wrought-iron gates of the winery and followed the winding driveway up to the main building. He left the car out front and went in to find Jon.

"Where's Mr. Woods?" Hudson asked Jessie, the part-time administrative assistant they'd hired to help with paperwork.

"In his office. He wants you to pop in."

Hudson entered Jon's neat-as-a-pin office. His partner sat behind an oak desk conversing with a blond man. Introductions were quickly made.

"Hudson, this is Scott Wilkinson. Scott's here to talk to us about the vineyard manager's job."

Manager's job? They'd talked briefly about hiring a seasoned professional to run their everyday business, but nothing concrete had been decided, at least nothing he remembered. They'd hoped that by bringing in someone who actually knew the wine industry inside and out, it would free them up to focus on their law practice. Right now that source of income was keeping them afloat.

Hudson went through the motions of shaking Wilkinson's hand. He listened, occasionally interjecting a question or two. From what he could gather, Scott Wilkinson was driving by, saw the Jon Hudson Cellars sign and decided to stop in. He'd just moved to Washington State from the Napa Valley where he'd managed a much larger winery than theirs. He was now looking for a position requiring less hours and felt a boutique winery might be the perfect fit.

"What are you expecting in terms of salary?" Jon asked, cutting to the chase.

Scott met Jon's gaze head-on. "In California I was making in the eighties."

Hudson kept a poker face. No way could they afford to pay that kind of salary. In the next month or so they'd have to hire a sales manager, and if they built a tasting room, that would also require a tasting-room manager. They were laying out far more than they were bringing in.

"We're a start-up outfit," Jon hastily explained. "We had our first crush last year. We're not exactly in the position to pay the kind of salary you made, at least not yet."

"I wasn't expecting you to," Scott answered gamely. "As I said before, I'm not looking to put in the long hours required at one of the bigger vineyards, which is why a place your size would work well for me."

He handed Jon a sealed envelope. "My résumé, see what you think."

More questions were asked, and at the end of the conversation Scott named a figure far less than had been previously mentioned, that he would be willing to take.

The interview concluded.

"Thanks for stopping by," Jon said. "I like what

I've heard so far. Hudson and I will talk it over and then get back to you in a few days."

"Your winery has a lot of potential," Scott said in parting. "Thanks for seeing me on very little notice."

When he was out of earshot, Jon glanced at his résumé before handing it to Hudson.

"Scott seems very well qualified and exactly what we need."

After a brief perusal of the man's curriculum vitae, Hudson agreed. "I don't think we can afford not to hire him."

He filled Jon in on his conversation with the banker.

"This guy really gets what we're doing," Hudson said. "He sees the potential for something big, and once he read our business plan he became even more enthusiastic. He didn't blink an eye when I felt him out about getting another loan."

"We've given four years of our lives to this place," Jon reminded him. "If it takes another loan to get us where we need to be, then I say do it."

"We've sunk over $600,000 into this venture, not including what we paid for the land. It's only money, right?"

"Yeah, right."

Hudson chuckled, but deep down he was worried, he'd never been this much in debt. True, the expense hadn't come as a complete surprise. They'd been warned by other viticulturists that growing grapes would initially be a labor of love. The first five years of start-up meant sinking money into the infrastructure. What they'd not been prepared for were vine damage due to frost and hail, mites, diseases and the supervision of a challenging, unionized workforce.

Hopefully the light at the end of the tunnel would come this spring with Jon Hudson's first release. It was something to look forward to, the culmination of a dream and a lot of personal sacrifice.

"I say we build a tasting room," his partner enthused. "Tasting rooms are supposedly a profit center. Not only do they serve an essential public-relations function, but they're a great place to promote wine club memberships."

"Well, another loan isn't going to make that much of a difference at this point," Hudson said, reluctantly, hating having such stifling debt.

"We gotta keep thinking big, bro. In another four to five years we'll be in the money, and you and I will be laughing about these lean days."

"I'll drink to that," Hudson answered, laughing and slapping his partner's back.

"Hell, no. I'm not about to have you drink up the profits."

Still laughing, both men went their separate ways.

Later that week, a male voice shouted from the dock, "Laila Stewart!"

Mariner's ears stood at full attention. A growl resounded from deep in his belly. He was instantly on alert anytime someone came within a few feet of *Copy Right*.

Peering through the peephole, Laila spotted a florist van parked on the dock. A delivery person armed with a huge bouquet was making his way toward the houseboat.

Mariner preceded Laila as she made her way down the gangway and toward the man. She accepted the cellophane-wrapped long-stemmed yellow roses, gave the delivery person a tip and retraced her steps. She sniffed the fragrant blooms before reading the card:

"Sorry I missed our anniversary. Please forgive me. Hudson."

That was that. No words of endearment. Yellow roses instead of red. Hudson was treating her like a friend, not a woman he cared deeply for.

She should feel elated by the arrangement, not sad. Except the flowers felt like a kiss-off, not the acknowledgment of a one-year milestone. If she hadn't reminded him, would he even have gone to the trouble?

Hearing his voice had started the familiar flutter of butterfly wings, although the conversation had left a lot to be desired.

She was getting it finally. She was not Hudson's top priority. Even when she'd taken the initiative and suggested she come to him, he'd brushed her off. Soon she would find out why his ardor had cooled.

Laila stuck the long-stemmed roses in a vase and placed them on her desk. She should call Hudson and thank him, but after their last conversation that wasn't about to happen. He either needed to work through his issues or communicate that their relationship was over.

When the phone rang Laila was certain that it was Hudson checking to see if she had received his flowers. To her disappointment it was a client wanting her to write a monthly newsletter for him. He was willing to pay good money, so why wasn't she more excited?

The phone rang again, and Laila considered letting the answering machine pick up. At the very last minute she grabbed the receiver.

"Laila Writes."

"May I speak with Laila Stewart, please?" a man's voice she didn't recognize inquired.

"This is she."

"Brock Lawrence here. We're supposed to be swapping homes."

"Thanks for the pictures, Brock. I love your cottage."

"I got yours, too. I didn't realize they made houseboats that nice. Love that rooftop garden."

"So are we still on for two weeks from today?"

"Yes, I'm all set to go."

They went over how finances would be handled and the length of the swap. Laila had already run a background check on Brock, and she was certain he'd done the same on her.

She picked up the receiver again, determined to thank Hudson for the roses and then set it down again. Let him call her. She had a good mind to thank him via e-mail, though that seemed so impersonal.

Either way, Hudson Godfrey was going to be in for the surprise of his life. What he didn't know was that Laila Stewart was coming to Washington State. She had a vested interest. Like it or not, he would have to deal with her.

Chapter 4

Laila's Blog
Monday, February 12

It took me almost a week to drive cross-country with frequent stops and having to find motels that would take Mariner. I did make reservations, but once the management saw the size of my beast several changed their minds.

It's been two whole days since I arrived on Whidbey Island and I'm already in love. The love bug bit from the moment I drove my Volkswagen Bug off the Mukilteo/Clinton ferry, and followed

Brock's directions. I immediately fell in love with Langley and its tiny permanent population of over one thousand. Brock's spacious cottage, which really is a converted barn, is like stepping into a postcard.

We drove through the most beautiful countryside to get here. Mariner, of course, immediately bounded out of the car and went off to christen Brock's backyard, leaving me to unload the vehicle. Men!

Carrying my boxes and bags under trellises covered with roses, I entered an artistically decorated cottage and raced up three little stairs to find the bedrooms.

Since then I've had two whole days to explore the nearby surroundings, and now I'm ready to venture out. Yes, I know it's two days before Valentine's Day and in exactly two hours Hudson Godfrey is about to get the surprise of his life.

Happy Valentine's Day, Hudson! Laila's arrived.

Laila had never done anything quite this bold ever, arriving on a man unannounced. Her justification was that a man who sent roses, and then didn't respond to the e-mail she sent to thank him, deserved anything he got. Besides, since she'd been hired by Jon Hudson why couldn't she just show up?

She'd gotten the directions to Jon Hudson

Cellars from MapQuest, and decided to leave Mariner behind. At the last minute she took a map with her, and right now that map was spread out on the VW's front seat. Fifteen minutes later she drove off the Mukilteo/Clinton ferry and took 525 South, which eventually would bring her to I405 South, which is where she needed to be.

The sky above was gray and the air blustery. It made Laila thankful for having worn a long-sleeved shirt under her black leather jacket. She'd donned stylish low-riser jeans with sensible ankle boots. When in Washington do as the Washingtonians do, except she had no intention of sacrificing her personal style. She'd be damned if she was going to see Hudson after all this time without looking good. Let him see what he was missing.

Despite the dank, gloomy day it was a picturesque drive but an unnerving one. In Florida she was used to driving on wide, flat highways, but there was nothing wide or flat about these hills, dales and hairpin bends. At times she found herself hanging on to her steering wheel for dear life.

About forty minutes later Laila entered the Sammamish River Valley. She followed the signs for Woodinville, and after driving up and down more winding roads finally entered the wrought-iron gates of Jon Hudson Cellars.

Laila followed the driveway until it dead-ended at a Victorian house. Taking a moment to compose herself, she glanced in the rearview mirror, making sure her mascara had not left her with raccoon eyes. She finger-fluffed her naturally curly hair, grabbed her purse and stepped out of the car. Taking a deep breath, she entered the building.

A young woman, who looked like she should still be in school, tore her eyes away from her computer monitor.

"May I help you?"

"I'm here to see Hudson Godfrey."

"Is Mr. Godfrey expecting you?"

"No. I'm an employee from out of town. If Hudson isn't here I'd like to see Jon."

"The owners are on the grounds. There was an emergency. One of the workers got hurt and they went off to see what they could do."

Talk about bad timing. Still, she'd come all this way and wasn't about to leave without at least letting Hudson know she was here. She was still standing, and it was evident that the secretary or whatever she was had no intention of inviting her to sit.

"I'll wait," Laila said, making herself comfortable in an uncomfortable-looking chair.

"And your name?" the woman/child asked, regarding her curiously.

"Laila."

The secretary's eyebrows shot to her hairline.

"Umm, let me see if I can get in touch with Mr. Godfrey." She reached for the phone.

"Someone looking for me?" Hudson's deep voice with its slight inflection came from behind Laila.

Even though it had been more than two months since she'd seen him, Laila reacted as she always had. The room had suddenly grown small and stifling. This must be what a hot flash felt like, she thought. Hudson's raw sexuality had always been a palpable thing. He still hadn't seen her, and Laila took a brief moment to examine him from head to toe.

If anything, Hudson was leaner but more muscular than she remembered. His skin, a rich mahogany, made his eyes seem even lighter. Hudson's broad, slightly flared nostrils and high cheekbones made him appear arrogant. His hair was trimmed close to his scalp making his features even more prominent. Under a heavy, midthigh jacket he wore Dockers and a long-sleeved polo shirt.

His secretary, using her head and flashing eyes, tried to send her boss a signal, one he just wasn't getting.

"Uh, you have a visitor," she finally said.

"I do?" Hudson's head swiveled and their eyes connected. "Laila! What are you doing here?"

She jumped up, quickly crossing the room to meet him. She'd expected to be swept into his arms, but Hudson remained still as a statue, his arms at his side.

"I thought I'd come and see what you're up to,"

Laila said, conscious of the secretary gaping. She stood on tiptoe kissing Hudson's cheek.

He'd never been one for public displays of affection, but a brush of the lips did not constitute a kiss as far as she was concerned. It was simply the way most people greeted each other. He took her elbow and marched her toward a closed door.

"You'll be more comfortable in my office."

Inside the cluttered room Hudson called an office, he swept aside papers and vine cuttings, plumped the cushion and waved her into a chair.

"You came all this way, why?" Hudson asked when they sat across from each other. He didn't sound particularly happy about it.

"Why wouldn't I?" Laila said.

"Where are you staying?"

"In a very nice cottage on Whidbey Island."

He narrowed his eyes. "Cottage? No hotel? Why Whidbey? How long will you be here?"

"You're full of questions. I'll be here five months and, no, no hotel. I swapped houses."

"You did what?"

Hudson made it sound as if she'd lost her mind. He didn't act or sound particularly happy to see her. Well, tough. There was nothing he could do now. She was here.

A series of raps on the door put an end to any further discussion. Jonathan Woods stuck his head in the crack.

"The paramedics are on their way, but I think our man will be all right. He's regained consciousness and seems to know where he is." His eyes grew round as he spotted Laila. "Hey, babe. Hudson, how come you didn't tell me your lady was coming?"

"Laila apparently wanted to surprise me." Hudson was all business again. "Hopefully there's nothing more wrong with that man except for having the wind knocked out of him. How could he possibly have fallen out of an ATV?"

"Was there an accident?" Laila asked as if she hadn't been clued in.

"Unfortunately, yes." Jonathan's voice grew grave. "Witnesses claimed one of our employees ran over some object and lost control. He fell from the vehicle."

"That's awful. What's an ATV?" Laila asked.

"All-terrain vehicle. It looks something like a minitractor or one of those sit-down lawn mowers. We use ATVs to get around the vineyard."

"What happens now?" Laila asked.

"We pray to God the man's really okay and hope he doesn't sue." Hudson was putting his worst fears into words.

"Why don't I accompany the injured man to the hospital while you take Laila out for a late lunch? It'll give you time to catch up. With Valentine's Day in just a couple of days, babe, now's the time to let this man know what you want." Jon winked at Laila. He headed out, adding, "Oh, and by the way, in case I miss you when I get back, leave me a number I can reach you. I want to talk to you about an upcoming event called Passport to Woodinville. We'll need you to write copy for us."

Laila was left facing Hudson alone.

"Let's get this lunch over with," he said, standing and towering over her. "I'll need to get back soon. I'm worried about my worker."

He'd been put on the spot. It certainly wasn't the most gracious invitation she'd ever received. In fact it wasn't an invitation at all. Hudson made taking her to lunch sound like an obligation. She'd come all this way, and this would be the first time in two months that they would be talking face-to-face. She wasn't about to miss out on this opportunity.

"Is there anything in particular you'd like to eat?" Hudson asked, his tone softening.

"I've been dying to try the famous clam chowder and the pan-fried oysters," Laila responded, following Hudson out.

"Nice car," she said, when she was seated in the Infiniti. "When did you get it?"

It occurred to her how very little she knew about a man she'd been intimate with for over a year. Their previous meet-ups had been in Fort Lauderdale on her turf, and she didn't have a clue how he lived.

"It's a lease," Hudson informed her. "I got the car about a year ago, around the same time I met you. It's an indulgence I write off on my taxes."

And he'd never once mentioned acquiring it. How strange and how unnecessarily secretive. What else was he keeping from her?

Hudson roared down the same driveway she'd come up less than an hour ago.

"How's business?" Laila asked, making conversation and hoping he would open up to her.

"Busy. I believe I mentioned our first release will be this spring. I'm hopefully optimistic that our Bordeaux will be well received, but it will be at least a couple more years before we actually see any money."

"But look at what you've accomplished in a relatively short time," Laila said, waving her hand with the discreet hummingbird tattoo at the wrist. "I was very impressed driving through the gates. Jon Hudson Cellars sounds and looks like a classy establishment."

"Humph! We're in debt up to our necks. I'll show you around when we get back."

"Getting a business onto firm ground takes time and costs money but the benefits of being your own boss can't be beat," she said sagely.

"True, but the headaches are all yours, as well."

Laila nodded her agreement. As far as she was concerned, not having a traditional boss to answer to more than made up for any of it. There had been days when she'd first launched Laila Writes that the phone hadn't rung once. She'd been panicked and desperate, knowing that her savings would only last so long. But at the same time, she'd been determined to be successful. Back then she'd never turned down a job, no matter how small it was. All that perseverance eventually paid off as she slowly built clientele. Jon Hudson would get there, too.

Jonathan was the person who'd initially asked her to write copy for them. After she'd been introduced to him in Fort Lauderdale, he'd called proposing she do some work for them. They'd conducted their business primarily over the phone. She'd sent samples of her work via e-mail, and whenever Hudson was on his way to and from visiting his family in Nassau, Bahamas, she would meet up with him. Theirs had been an instant attraction that blossomed into a full-fledged affair, albeit a long-distance one.

In so many ways they were a perfect match. Hudson was busy and she was busy, so long-distance worked well for both of them, or so she'd thought. But as time went by, Laila became more frustrated. She felt that the relationship was based on convenience—Hudson's convenience, that is.

"Another five minutes and we're there," he said, driving down a one-way street at breakneck speed.

Soon they turned off the main thoroughfare and

crunched their way up a gravel-strewn driveway. Hudson brought the car to a halt in front of what appeared to be a converted barn, and turned the vehicle over to a waiting valet.

As he helped Laila out of the car and their fingers linked, the old magic returned. Laila's body began pulsating in places it shouldn't have. This wasn't good.

They were taken to a table in the back of the main dining area. In keeping with the rustic setting, quilts hung from the walls and antiques were scattered throughout. Reminders that soon it would be Valentine's Day were all around: spiraling hearts hung from the vaulted ceiling, and large Hershey's Kisses dominated corners. An aging pianist provided mood music, playing on an even older upright piano. His specialty was old Billie Holiday tunes.

Once water was poured and orders taken, Hudson scrutinized Laila with those light eyes of his.

"Why did you really come to Washington, Laila?" he asked.

She fiddled with the cloth napkin in her lap, choosing her words carefully. "I needed a change. When an opportunity to swap residences presented itself, I took advantage of it."

"And you never once mentioned you'd be here. Why not California or Georgia?"

What was it with him?

"You were here, for one. You sound upset that I came."

"Not upset. I just don't have a lot of time at my disposal to spend with you. You'll feel neglected."

Hudson was making it clear that if she expected more of him, he wasn't prepared to give it.

"Are we officially breaking up, then?" she asked.

Hudson sipped on his water, avoiding her gaze. She'd gotten her answer loud and clear.

"Laila, we were never that serious to begin with."

Bastard! She tried for a watery smile. She would not break down, would not give him the satisfaction of letting him know just how much he'd hurt her.

"Are you saying that for the past year or so we've been having a fling?" she asked.

"Now, you know that's not been the case."

"Then what was it, then?"

"We enjoyed each other's company. You and I also had a business arrangement."

She felt as if someone had put an ice pick to her heart.

Hudson reached across the table and covered her hand with his. Under the table her knees began knocking so hard she hoped he couldn't tell. Thankfully their food arrived and there was something else to concentrate on.

"Is there someone else?" Laila asked, forcing her voice to remain steady. She raised her fork in a valiant attempt to eat, though truthfully she'd lost her appetite.

"No. But building a business is a demanding mistress. Right now I need to focus all my energy on the winery."

She was being dumped, and according to him the competition was work. There was nothing left to say. He'd made his choice—work, not her—and she wasn't about to grovel. She also wasn't about to walk away from the work that he and Jon had contracted her for.

When the silence stretched out Hudson added, "What I'm saying is I'd like to put our relationship on hold for now."

Laila bit back the hot retort on the tip of her tongue. On hold? The colossal gall of him, did he really think she was going to sit around waiting for him to determine when it was right to resume their involvement?

"No matter how you put it, we're breaking up, Hudson," she said firmly. "This clearly isn't working for either of us."

"I value your friendship, Laila. You're a decent woman."

She wanted to scream out her frustration.

"I value our business relationship," she countered. "Jon's mentioned that he's got some work he'd like me to do. Perhaps we should stick to business and discuss this in greater detail."

Ironic that two days before Valentine's Day she was being cut loose. It wasn't as if she hadn't seen it coming.

It was going to be some fun Valentine's Day. What a welcome to Washington this had turned out to be.

Chapter 5

"That's one helluva together woman you hooked up with," Jon said as they perched on bar stools at the neighborhood brewery, chugging a couple of cold ones. "I wish I could find one just like her."

"Laila and I are no longer a couple. Hopefully we can remain friends," Hudson answered.

Over the neck of his beer bottle Jon gave him a narrow-eyed stare. "You're one crazy dude. That woman is prime rib."

"Don't you think I know that? But I can't be involved right now. It's not fair to her. Not until the business is on more stable ground."

Hudson guessed Jon would be all over him when

he found out he'd broken things off. He'd often suspected his partner had a thing for Laila. Jon had made no secret he thought she was hot. What's more, he respected her and thought she was one of the most talented copywriters around.

"You just made one of the biggest mistakes of your life, bro," Jon confirmed. "Quality women are hard to find."

"You should talk. You can't even remember the last time you dated."

"I'm just being selective. My tolerance for drama is nil."

Not wanting the conversation to continue in this vein, Hudson scanned the crowd. The bar was packed with casually but professionally dressed patrons on their way home from work. The majority were information-technology types, judging by the conversations he overheard.

He and Jon had needed to unwind after a stressful day. Their injured employee had nothing seriously wrong with him other than a couple of bumps and bruises. It was now left to be seen whether or not he would sue.

What really tore up Hudson was breaking up with Laila. Although it had been a long time in coming, he hadn't handled the situation well. But all things considered, she'd been gracious and hadn't thrown a fit. She'd surprised him by coming all this way from Fort Lauderdale, and he hadn't known how to deal with it.

Now that it was done and over with he could fully concentrate on the business. But deep down he felt lousy. The alcohol was doing nothing to soothe his guilty conscience or erase the memories of the hurt reflected in Laila's wide brown eyes.

"Anything you want to talk about?" Jon asked, waving a hand in front of his face.

"Yes, as a matter of fact, there is. We should talk about getting Scott Wilkinson on board as soon as we can. With the kind of case load we're both handling, we need someone ASAP—a person who can give one hundred percent of their time to production."

For the next fifteen minutes the men discussed their finances and the need for additional personnel. At the end of the conversation they'd more than justified going ahead and applying for that loan.

"I'm going to take off," Jon said, slapping a couple of crisp bills down on the bar. "I'd like to be straight with you, though, so you don't think I'm doing anything underhanded. I'm going to call Laila and ask her to dinner. I don't think it's right that she is left to her own devices on Valentine's night." He held up his hand, stopping Hudson from interrupting. "Don't worry. I'll make sure she understands this is a business dinner. We've always enjoyed each other's company, so it definitely won't be a hardship on my part. And she does work for us."

Although Hudson had been the one to engineer the breakup, he was still ticked. Given the number of single women in the Sammamish Valley that Jon could take out on Valentine's night, he'd chosen Laila. Something seemed off with that.

When her cell phone rang, Laila debated picking up. She didn't recognize the incoming caller but hesitated about letting the call go to voice mail. It just might be a client.

"Laila Writes," she answered.

"Hi, hon. How are you doing?" The male voice was one she couldn't immediately identify.

"Who is this?"

"Jonathan Woods."

"Oh, Jon. Sorry about that. I guess I wasn't expecting to hear from you."

"I wanted to catch you before you made other plans. I was thinking that we might have dinner the day after next?"

"On Valentine's night?" Her voice sounded too high.

"Yes, ma'am. Hudson told me you and he broke up. I'm here to offer you a shoulder to lean on. I thought we could keep each other company and get some business done at the same time."

Dinner with Jon sounded inviting. Laila had

always liked him, and it was certainly a better alternative than sitting around feeling sorry for herself. She'd decided for the next five months she'd bury herself in work, and when time permitted she'd do some exploring of the beautiful countryside. There was so much she wanted to see.

"Give me your address and I'll come by around seven to pick you up," Jon said.

Laila gave him the information and then hung up feeling much happier. Jon Woods had always treated her with the utmost respect. He was a good friend and right now she could use one.

A cold nose nudged Laila's shin. She reached over to scratch Mariner behind the ear. The dog, always in tune with her moods, plopped down on her feet. He must have sensed she was a little off today.

In some ways it was good knowing where she stood with Hudson. They'd never discussed a future together, but he'd been an integral part of her life for over a year. She was comfortable with him and used to his ways. Now it seemed strange to suddenly be free again. She should have felt liberated; instead she felt weird.

At least now she could explore what was out there. She'd run into a few men on her morning walks. Most were the outdoors type and in great physical shape. Jon wasn't exactly what you'd call chopped liver, either, but the two men were business partners and friends, and that presented problems.

For the next two days Laila familiarized herself with the little town. She decided if she was going to be on Whidbey Island for the next few months, then she'd better make the most of it.

On one of her walks she came upon an outdoor café that attracted an interesting cross section of people, primarily dog lovers. The animals contentedly lounged at their owners' feet, ears up, listening to the animated conversations surrounding them. Out of sheer curiosity, Laila wandered in with Mariner.

"I haven't seen you around before," the blonde who poured her coffee said.

"That's because I've only been here a few days," Laila answered, smiling back at the server.

"Where do you come from?"

"Fort Lauderdale."

"That's a long ways away," a woman seated at an adjacent table leaned over, interjecting. She looked to be of mixed race. "Would you like to join me?"

"I'd love to."

At the woman's feet was a hyper Chihuahua who kept circling. Mariner's tail was thumping like crazy, and Laila guessed the little dog was female.

The server helped Laila move her coffee to her new friend's table.

"I'm Dara and this is Fiesta," the light-skinned

woman with uncontrollable bouncy brown hair began. “Is that beautiful dog a boy or girl?”

“Mariner’s a boy. And yours?”

“Fiesta is definitely a girl and a huge flirt. How come I haven’t seen you before?”

“Because I’ve just moved here.”

Laila explained about the house swap.

“How cool! There aren’t too many of us living on Whidbey Island,” Dara confided, lowering her voice and confirming her ethnicity. “How come you moved here of all places?”

Laila explained she was a freelance copywriter. For some inexplicable reason she felt comfortable sharing why she’d come to Washington on a whim and why she’d felt the need to find out what Hudson was up to.

“And what did you find?” Dara asked, her gray eyes widening with curiosity.

“I confirmed what I knew in my gut. He no longer wanted to continue the relationship.”

“That’s got to be tough.”

“Nothing I can’t handle.” Laila tried for a bright smile. “I’d suspected he wanted out for a while, but now rather than guessing I have closure. What do you do?”

“I play violin with the symphony.”

“As in the Seattle Symphony? How cool.”

“I love what I do.”

For the next half hour Dara regaled her with outrageous stories of life on Whidbey, and the colorful characters that lived on the island. It turned out the two women had a lot in common, including having similar upbringings. Both were children of navy men and used to picking up and moving on a whim. Finally they exchanged phone numbers and Laila prepared to head off.

"You can find me here most mornings," Dara shouted over Fiesta's high-pitched keening. The Chihuahua was already having separation anxiety. "There's also a copywriting group that you might want to join."

"Call me and we'll schedule another time to get together," Laila suggested, making a motion with her hands. Mariner meanwhile barked a fond farewell to his friend.

Two days later Laila was all dressed up and waiting for Jon to pick her up. He'd made reservations at a restaurant in Seattle overlooking the sound.

Laila was looking forward to their evening out. So far Valentine's Day had really sucked. All day long Laila had been forced to watch delivery vans wind their way up the mountainous roads laden with goodies. She'd tried her best not to dwell on the fact that there would be no flowers for her today, not even the yellow roses that she loved. She'd not expected to be this upset. It wasn't as if she hadn't seen the breakup coming.

Mariner lay on the couch, his big black nose

pressed against the glass pane, woofing and drooled intermittently. Jon must be here.

Laila opened the door to a well-dressed Jon. He thrust a red rose at her. She'd always thought him handsome, but to her mind Hudson was the better looking of the two. Jon was more muscular than his partner. He had bitter-chocolate skin and a goatee that he kept neatly trimmed.

"Happy Valentine's Day, sweetie," he said, kissing her cheek and handing her a box of truffles. "By the way, the chocolates are compliments of Hudson."

"Why would he do that?"

"Why would he not?"

"We broke up."

Jon draped an arm around her shoulders. "That doesn't mean he stopped caring about you. I hope you're hungry. We'll talk more over dinner."

Carrying her rose with her, Laila followed Jon out to his sport-utility vehicle. They caught the ferry with just minutes to spare, and after a half-hour drive arrived at the restaurant.

"This is great," Laila gushed when they were seated at a table with a wonderful view of the sound.

The establishment was a popular one and packed with couples, some on dates and others appeared to be regulars clearly taken with the food.

"It's one of my favorite restaurants," Jon admitted. "Hudson and I have business meetings here. Usually we get our choice of tables."

Jon had to bring him up. Where was Hudson? Was he home alone or out with her replacement? She didn't want to think about him being with another woman. She was determined to enjoy Jon's company and hear more about the work they were here to discuss.

"Laila, you're a million miles away," Jon said, waving his hand in front of her face as she stared off into the distance.

"What? Sorry."

"I was asking how you felt about coming in to work at the winery, a couple of days a week?"

Laila scrunched up her nose.

"I'm not sure that's a good idea."

"Why, because of Hudson? Put him aside and put on your business hat. As I mentioned before I'm not happy with the content on the Web site. I'd like to have the whole thing rewritten and post some more enticing pictures. This is where your graphic design and copywriting skills come into play. I also need you to design a label for the bottles and flyers we hand out. We're also discussing distributing a monthly newsletter, as well. There's plenty of work to do."

"Work that doesn't require me being on the property. Why do I need to be on the premises to write copy?" Laila asked, an eyebrow raised. Seeing Hudson every day would be agony.

"Because you need to get a real feel for the business. It just translates to better copy. Think of those royalties we've offered you on future wine sales. They could be quite considerable once the winery takes off."

Laila felt the tug of temptation. Those royalties could make a big difference in her life, and the exposure could put her in the league of master copywriters. Laila had always wanted to set up a scholarship for underprivileged youth who dared to dream. While she lived comfortably, she'd never had excess money to do something really philanthropic. Going to the vineyard might also help put structure to her week. But could she deal with running into Hudson?

"Let me think about it," she said, not wanting to appear too eager.

The waiter chose that moment to appear and take their orders.

"Why aren't you out tonight with your significant other?" she asked the moment the server was out of earshot.

Jon smiled enigmatically. "What brought that up?"

"It's Valentine's night and we're not exactly a couple."

"Ever thought you might be doing me a favor, keeping me from getting depressed?"

Laila blinked away the moisture gathered in the

corners of her eyes. Jon had been doing a good job of keeping her engaged until now. She would have a good time if it killed her.

Buying herself time, she gazed around the crowded room. The stem of the wineglass almost snapped as she spotted the couple on the far side of the room.

"Why that rotten, lying bastard," she muttered through clenched teeth.

"Have I offended you?"

Jonathan gazed in the direction she was looking. A man who looked a lot like Hudson had his head inches away from a woman with a mane of hair and the contents of an entire cosmetic counter on her face. A polished fingernail tapped Hudson's cheek.

"Oops! Not good. I had no idea Hudson would be here," Jon confirmed gently. "We can leave if you'd like."

"No. Why leave? I'm going to pretend that I don't even see them."

"Talia Chisolm is one of Hudson's clients. He's representing her in a very nasty divorce," Jon explained, taking Laila's hand as if that would ease the pain.

"No need to explain anything to me. Hudson and I are no longer going out, remember?"

Then why did it hurt so much seeing him with another woman? And why had she just made up her mind to accept Jon's offer to come into the winery and work?

She wouldn't fall apart because Hudson Godfrey had decided she was not what he wanted. There were plenty of other fish in the sea.

It was high time to go fishing.

Chapter 6

Dumb! Dumb! Dumb! Hudson chastised himself for not checking with Jon to find out where he was having dinner. How mortifying and embarrassing to end up at the same place as Laila and Jon. It wasn't as if he was out having a romantic dinner, either. Talia Chisolm was a client, and a damn difficult one at that.

Hudson's concentration was totally thrown now. He should be focusing on Talia and her woes, not darting looks in the corner where Jon and Laila sat. Laila was stunning tonight, not that she wasn't always stunning. She had her naturally curly hair pulled off her face, a scarf securing it back. The simple black dress she wore with a silver necklace suited her personality. There were never any pretensions with Laila, and tonight she stood out in the garden of women dressed in red and pink.

Hudson trusted Jon, although the two seemed absorbed in each other. He'd been concerned that he'd broken Laila's heart, but she seemed to be doing just fine. Pssshht! She'd been all he'd been able to think about since that awful conversation, and now seeing Laila in person made him have many regrets. He was an idiot for giving her up. The moment his gaze had locked with hers, he'd tuned out Talia Chisolm, demanding as she was.

Hudson made himself bring his focus back. He was being paid by the hour to listen.

"What am I going to do for money until this marriage is over with?" Talia Chisolm carped. "Brandon's cleaned out every checking account and he's closed our savings. I'm left with nothing."

Nothing other than the two-million-dollar house on Lake Washington you still live in and Brandon paid for, and the household expenses your husband is still picking up.

"I'm working on getting you a temporary order," he said, keeping his own counsel. "Did I misunderstand you, or did you not tell me that you had a separate bank account in addition to your joint funds?"

"I have an account. But I am used to a certain standard of living. I have two kids to raise, and I've never been able to work. What little money I have is almost gone, and yet Brandon gets to spend our money on his little ho."

Hudson took a deep breath and prepared for the histrionics.

"Didn't you tell me your husband pays child support religiously?"

"Yes, but that money's for the children. What about me?"

Talia required patience. Hudson took another deep breath. It was going to be one long night. Patience and diplomacy came with the territory. Hudson had chosen family law because it provided a nice steady source of income. He liked representing spouses who were being taken advantage of by their partners.

His father had been one of those men who'd gotten a raw deal. He'd survived with not one dollar of child support after Hudson's mother had run off with a man she felt could provide for her better.

Talia Chisolm, however, was a whole other story. She was tough as nails and shrewd as they come. Her husband, Brandon, had dumped her for another piece of arm candy, and now Talia was determined to make him pay for her embarrassment in cold, hard cash. Hudson suspected Talia already had the next Mr. Chisolm lined up.

"Why do you keep looking off in that corner?" Talia asked, her voice grating on his nerves. "Do you see someone you know? What are you doing conducting business on Valentine's night, anyway? Don't you have a honey?"

The conversation was getting way too personal for Hudson's liking. He gave Talia a tight smile and then followed with the party line.

"My clients are always a top priority."

Talia wasn't buying any of it.

"A young, hot, virile guy like you must have someone. If not it's your own doing," she said. "You could have any woman in this place."

Hudson tried not to groan out loud.

"My focus right now is on getting you the kind of settlement you are entitled to. Brandon's attorney placed another offer on the table. He'd prefer not to go to court and have both of your names dragged through the mud. He's thinking of the children."

"He's thinking of himself," Talia said, leaning over and using her finger to brush a crumb off of his lips. "And I need to think about myself. What exactly is the old geezer proposing?"

Hudson discussed the terms of the proposal. Privately he thought it was a rather generous settlement. Talia, of course, would expect more.

She laughed raucously.

"Forget about it. The man's worth a bundle. He'll need to have to cough up a heck of a lot more dollars, and there is the matter of that Ferrari he promised to buy me but never did. No way am I being left out in the cold."

Hudson was slowly starting to lose patience with Talia. She was his client, but she was being totally unreasonable. He was actually quite happy when he saw Jon heading his way. He hoped Jon was coming over to extend an invitation to join him and Laila for dessert.

Perhaps it was wishful thinking on his part, but it sure would make his Valentine's Day.

Laila's Blog
Wednesday, February 14

Valentine's Day, actually it's Valentine's night. It's been a fiasco so far. Seeing Hudson with some cougar—she had to be forty if she was a day—was like getting an ice pick through my heart. Of course Hudson pretended not to see me, but what else could he do?

He could hardly leave his girlfriend sitting at the table and come over to say hello. I would probably have lost it anyway, and dumped a glass of water over his head, the two-timing bastard. Jon, as usual, was full of excuses for his buddy. He made up a story that the woman who looked like an advertisement for a cosmetic company was a client. Did he really expect me to believe it? The client was not only hanging out, but hanging all over him.

No client I know of rims a finger around some man's lips. And the getup said client was wearing would have anyone hot. I'll never trust another man again, at least not with my heart. My mother warned me about men like him. She said they were all liars, and she should know.

My father left us high and dry after my mom gave him fifteen years of her life. She followed him all over the globe and back, giving up a successful career in banking to be a homemaker. And now his current wife was exactly what he said he didn't want—a high-powered executive who didn't have the inclination to boil water.

What was the point of rehashing a relationship that didn't work? I'm long over Hudson Godfrey and his two-timing ways! I hope the two of them have a nice life together.

Two days later Laila drove her car off the Whidbey Island ferry and headed for Woodinville. She'd now had time to think and wasn't so sure she was completely over Hudson. In fact, she hoped she didn't run into him. She was going to the winery at his partner's request. Jon had scheduled the meeting and she was anxious to hear what he had to say.

As luck would have it, just as Laila pulled the Volkswagen up to the curb, Hudson emerged from the Victorian house that was the main building. He had a tall blond man with him.

"Hi, Laila," he greeted, as if seeing her on his premises was an everyday thing. "Jon did say you might stop by. Have you met Scott Wilkinson, our newly hired vineyard manager?"

"No, I haven't." Laila shook the hand the blond man held out. "Nice meeting you, Scott. Best of luck to you."

"Thank you, Laila."

"Jon's in his office," Hudson said, making a U-turn. "Do you need me to show you where he is?"

She didn't need him to show her anything. She shook her head.

"I'll catch up with you later, Scott," he said over his shoulder, ignoring her completely. Hudson headed back inside and led her down a long hallway. "How's it going? Have you settled into your new home?"

"I'm unpacked and I've met a few people." She hoped the tremors on the inside weren't showing on the outside.

"You've made friends, then?" Hudson asked, fishing.

Laila decided to keep him guessing. "You could say that. I've met some nice people with whom I have something in common."

"If you ever have free time I'll be happy to show you around," Hudson offered. "I've lived most of my life in Washington State."

A gracious offer but one probably made out of guilt…guilt or obligation.

"It's beautiful country, but I don't know how it could possibly compare to the Bahamas where you were born," Laila countered.

"Both have their good points."

They entered Jon's office to find him on the phone. He smiled at them and raised a finger in the air, signaling that he would be with them shortly.

Laila and Hudson slid into the seats facing him.

Jon's office was the exact opposite of Hudson's. He was as neat as they come and had a place for everything. When he set the phone back in its cradle he stepped out from behind his desk and held his arms wide.

"You look great!" he said. "Want to see what we've done with the place?"

"We'll both show Laila around," Hudson was quick to say. "Scott's okay on his own for the next hour or so."

Hudson was sending her confusing signals, but maybe it was his way of being friendly since the relation was now a business one. In essence she was his employee.

She was whisked through the Victorian home and then taken through the outer buildings. Laila visited the production, bottling and barreling room, watching in awe the wine being aged in huge oak barrels, all in preparation for the first release.

"This is where we want to build our tasting room," Hudson said, pointing to a spot with a wonderful view of the Cascade Mountains. "Just imagine sipping wine and looking out onto those awesome mountains. Want to see where we grow some of our grapes?"

Hudson's and Jon's enthusiasm began slowly rubbing off. Laila felt her own excitement build as they shared their dreams for Jon Hudson Cellars.

Outside, the cool winter air added a spring to her step. Being close to Hudson was an invigorating high and could easily be addictive.

"Take the Jeep and I'll drive the ATV and catch up with Scott," Jon offered.

Mention of the ATV brought to mind the injured worker.

"How is that man, the one who fell off the equipment?" Laila asked.

"He had a few minor cuts and bruises. We gave him a couple of weeks off with pay. More out of goodwill than anything else."

"Well, I'm off," Jon said, hopping into the ATV's seat. "You two can discuss what copy we'll need while you do your little tour."

"Jon…"

But Jon was already zipping off, leaving her alone with Hudson. Well, almost alone, except for the workers busy with their own chores.

Electrical bolts surged through her body, although she tried her best to appear cool.

"Did I mention how nice you looked the other

night?" Hudson asked, sending her over the top. The compliment came totally out of left field.

Laila's shapeless, hooded sweatshirt wasn't exactly the height of fashion, but it was warm, comfortable and perfect for touring the cellars and outdoors.

"What was I wearing?" Laila asked, trying to recall what she'd thrown on hastily before Jon showed up.

"A black dress that suited you perfectly. You were the epitome of elegance."

"Thank you, that was nice of you to notice."

How formal they'd become.

"You were hard to miss," Hudson flirted. He flicked her wrist with his finger. "Nice bracelet. Remember when I gave you that charm?" Hudson touched a miniature gold pen that he'd given her to celebrate a particularly lucrative deal. Ten thousand dollars wasn't exactly chump change to a copywriter trying to get a business up and running.

Laila playfully jangled her wrist at him. While she had no desire to take a walk down memory lane with him, she was eating up the compliments.

The conversation took a different turn as they drove down more dirt roads. Hudson proudly pointed out the areas he'd designated for grape growing.

"Ultimately I'd like to grow all of our grapes in one spot and not have to buy vines from other vintners," he said wistfully.

"And you will. Everything in its own time."

Hudson's gaze locked with hers before his attention returned to the dirt road.

"You've always been my biggest champion."

"I've always believed in you, but that wasn't enough."

She could have slapped herself the moment the words slipped out. She sounded bitter and like a whining shrew. But she was falling under Hudson's spell again, hanging on to his every word.

Hudson began talking about what a labor of love it had taken to get him here. The pride in his voice tore at her insides as he recounted the challenges of starting up a winery and all the problems he and Jon had overcome to date.

She was fascinated and intrigued by his stories of mishaps and misfortunes. Yet they'd persisted and thrived until Jon Hudson Cellars materialized. Now her heart was on guard and she had no intention of getting caught up in Hudson's madness again. Now it was safer to stick to business and the real reason she was here.

"Jon mentioned there were several pieces of copy you'd like me to write," Laila said. "Have you thought about what you want?"

"We've been talking about a newsletter, maybe a monthly release to educate people on different Washington wines. Most people don't realize that pricey doesn't necessarily mean good."

"Yes, Jon did mention something about it. He

also asked me about designing a label for your wine bottles."

Hudson was back to business now. His professional demeanor made things so much easier.

"Yes, the label will need to be designed soon. I'd hoped for something classy but fun, something that will catch the eye of a younger professional crowd…and those with disposable incomes. The copy on our Web site also needs to be updated. I wrote it, and frankly it's bone dry and sounds a lot like legalese."

Hudson laughed out loud. He did have a sense of humor, and that was another thing Laila liked about him.

"It's that bad, huh?" she said, chuckling. "I'll take a look and see what I can do to loosen things up. Aren't you glad that you and I can laugh about these things?"

"We've always shared the same sense of humor," Hudson answered. "I'm glad you're here."

He liked having her here. He just didn't care to be romantically involved with her.

It confused her, this chemistry between them. Yet there was nothing to indicate Hudson regretted ending the relationship.

He reached over and tucked a wisp of escaping hair behind her ear. Another mistake.

"Laila?" he whispered.

"What, Hudson?"

Hudson's face was only inches from hers. She couldn't resist outlining his lips with her fingers. He parted them to nibble on her index and middle finger. She was already breathing hard, practically panting. It triggered an electric reaction and soon they were kissing.

Laila couldn't get enough of him. Hudson smelled and tasted like a full-bodied red wine but far more heady and intoxicating than any she'd tasted. His tongue rimmed her mouth and she opened up to let him in.

Ripples of sensations rushed through Laila. Every sense was on alert. She'd always thought of Hudson as eye candy, and just looking at him could get her going. Laila wrapped her arms around his long, lean body and felt the sinew and muscles bunch in his back. Only seconds into the kiss and she was ready to take things to another level.

When Hudson thrust his tongue farther into Laila's mouth, she heard his sharp intake of breath. She held on to his tongue, relishing the fruity taste. Hudson tasted far better than any aging Bordeaux. She'd missed him and the uninhibited sex that came with being comfortable. It had made the wait between visits more bearable.

A rap on the window caused them to slide apart. How embarrassing to have been caught groping as if they were two overheated teenagers? Hudson rolled down his window and stuck his head out.

"Is there a problem?" he asked the man who was standing there practically hopping from one foot to the other.

"Yes, there is, sir. I need you to come with me right away."

Chapter 7

"Suppose you tell me what's going on?" Hudson asked.

The laborer wiped his face on a soiled handkerchief he took from his pocket. Despite the chill in the air, a thin layer of perspiration coated his forehead. He was still trying to catch his breath and looked as if he'd been running.

"I will explain as we go along. It is important you come now before the men walk off the job."

"Get in, Luis," Hudson ordered, opening up the back door of the vehicle. The worker quickly scrambled in. "Why would they do that?"

"The men claim they make more money at one of

the bigger vineyards. A man, he show up earlier telling everyone to come and work for him. He say he pay by the day, and he say he always pays in cash."

Hudson put the vehicle in gear. "How come you haven't taken him up on his offer, then? How come you stayed, Luis?"

"Because I work for you for a long time. You treat me well. You pay on time. I feel…" His hand clutched his heart.

"Loyalty?" Hudson finished.

"Yes, loyalty, so I come to tell you so that you not surprised. If you pay more, or maybe match the money, we all stay and you have labor force."

Hudson remained silent for a while, digesting what his employee said.

"Have you spoken to your new boss, Mr. Wilkinson? Does he know there's a problem?"

"Yes, yes, he is talking to the men right now, but they not know him, maybe don't trust him. You need to come. The workers, the ones that are left will want to hear from you."

"Okay, I'm on my way," Hudson said, flooring the accelerator. "Show me where this gathering is."

"In the opposite direction. Turn around, sir, and go back a little."

Hudson did a quick U-turn and followed Luis's directions. A few minutes later he pulled off to the side of the road, parking in front of one of the outbuildings.

Judging by the wild gesticulations there seemed to be an uprising in the making. A small group of workers circled Jon and the newly hired manager. Angry words were being yelled in Spanglish and English.

"What is going on?" Hudson yelled, striding into the middle of the group while Laila remained in the vehicle. This wasn't her fight and frankly none of her business.

Hudson's arrival put an end to the angry threats, although some muttering could still be heard.

"Okay, who wants to talk to me?"

Again no one spoke up. Scott and Jon now flanked him, providing support. The employee who'd tipped Hudson off, afraid of being labeled a snitch, was hunkering down in the backseat.

"We want more money to keep working," one of the workers said after being prompted by his coworkers.

"Yeah!" the unified group yelled.

"You're paid a fair wage. We researched the going rate and I'm confident we match what everyone else is paying," Hudson returned.

"No, you don't. We can barely feed our families," another worker shouted. "Linton Estates pays almost one dollar more per hour. Why should we stay with you?"

"We've always taken care of you," Jonathan pointed out. "Does Linton Estates offer their vineyard staff health benefits and a 401(k) retirement plan?"

That silenced the group momentarily, but soon they regrouped and began to mumble amongst themselves.

A large African-American man shouted, "Okay but what about cold hard cash in our pockets, boss? We all have bills to pay."

Scott Wilkinson stepped forward, palms in the air, waiting for the group to quiet down.

"Listen to what you're saying. Aren't health benefits valuable? Could you pay for them on your own? All we do is take a tiny deduction out of your checks and we supplement the difference. You don't think that's worth more than one dollar an hour?

"I bet you Linton doesn't pick up the tab for their employees' health. Before you make your move you'd better figure out what you're going to do if your wife gets sick. Or, God forbid, your child has an accident? Will the eight extra dollars a day take care of that hospital bill?"

The group began talking over each other, trying to decide whether Scott made sense.

Initially Laila thought Scott was being unnecessarily harsh, but as the muttering grew louder, she realized that the frank, straightforward approach seemed to work with this crowd.

She was impressed that Jon and Hudson had taken care of their workers. It must be costing them a bundle. Unfortunately, the generous gesture didn't seem appreciated by these men. She was so tempted to climb out of the SUV and slap some sense into them.

"You make a good point, boss," one of the more sensible men eventually said. "I guess we got carried away by the instant money."

"If you choose to leave we will not be taking you back," Scott warned. "Please get that word out to those who've already left. There will be no coming back."

The group seemed stunned by their manager's announcement. The mutterings ceased. Hudson and Jon nodded in support, allowing Scott to take over the show.

"Okay, now that we understand each other, here's the plan," Scott said. "Talk to your buddies looking for a job and tell them about our medical benefits and our retirement plan. If anyone you recommend gets hired, we'll give you a monetary incentive for bringing them on board. Now back to work everyone. This little uprising can't continue on Jon Hudson Cellars' time."

The men quickly dispersed, and the management team huddled. Finally Hudson returned to the truck.

"Everything okay?" Laila asked when he was again behind the wheel.

"For now, anyway. Our new manager did an

awesome job of putting things into perspective for the men, didn't you think?"

"I thought *you* did an awesome job."

Hudson turned to Luis, still crouched down in the backseat. "Where would you like me to drop you off?"

"Anywhere my friends can't see me, or there will be trouble."

"You got it."

Hudson let Luis off on a side road close to where he'd been found. When he pulled up in front of the main building Jon was already there.

"Let's hope that's the last of our labor problems," he said to his partner as he helped Laila out of the vehicle.

"Scott has already more than earned his money, as far as I'm concerned," Jon responded.

"I'd be real interested in seeing how many workers we pick up from our new employee-referral program. We'll have to put our heads together and come up with an appropriate incentive reward."

"For the workers or Scott?" Jon shot back.

The men laughed and slapped each other on the back. Laila cleared her throat, reminding them that she was still around.

"I'm going to take off," she interjected.

Hudson placed a steadying hand on her arm. "Hang out for a few more minutes. We still need to come up with a game plan and establish deadlines for the copy, et cetera. And you need to know how you'll be paid."

"I spoke to Laila about coming in a few days a week," Jon said, "at least to start with. I've offered royalties as part of her compensation package."

"Then we'll need just a few more minutes of her time to nail down all the particulars."

The meeting had already eaten up the better part of Laila's day. There was Mariner to worry about. In retrospect she probably should have brought the dog with her. He wasn't used to being left alone for any length of time.

Laila listened to the men discuss their vision for Jon Hudson Cellars. They brainstormed a design for the wine bottle labels and then discussed the format and layout for the monthly newsletter.

"We'll need to start advertising the tasting room soon," Hudson added. "It's going to take the better part of two months to construct, but it should be up and running by the time our first wines are released."

"This is all very exciting but I need to get home," Laila said, fumbling through her purse to find her keys. "I've got Mariner to get back to. Most of my writing can be done out of the house. However, on the days I come in I'd like to bring him with me. Is that a problem?"

"I don't see it as one. Do you, Jon? Mariner is very welcome. He's a great dog."

Hudson and her mastiff had a special bond, and that was an additional reason why their breakup was tough.

"We'll see both of you in a couple of days," Hudson said, walking her to where the Volkswagen was parked.

"I'll find you a little cubbyhole to work out of," Jon called after her. "It's good to have you here."

"Thanks, Jon. I'll start working on some ideas so that we have something to discuss the next time around."

Being with Hudson for an extended period of time had thrown her totally off-kilter. Needing a distraction, she checked her cell phone for messages. On Whidbey Island there were areas where cell service was spotty or nonexistent. Dara had left a message asking Laila to join her for happy hour at a bar in Oak Harbor. She mentioned she'd be there with a group of artsy friends.

Two hours later Laila, with Mariner in the passenger seat, navigated the winding roads to Oak Harbor. A steady drizzle prevented it from being a picturesque drive. Oak Harbor was the largest city on Whidbey Island, and Laila had read somewhere it was named for the Garry oak trees that graced its skyline.

The city had a population of over twenty thousand people, and the naval station on the outskirts brought with it a diverse population. By the time Laila found the bar nestled on the shores of Puget Sound, a heavy fog had rolled in, obscuring what must be an awesome view of the water.

She put Mariner on his leash before entering the building. Inside, a good-size crowd of casually dressed people were downing beers and making the rounds. Laila kept an eye out for Dara but didn't immediately see anyone with bouncy curls and an out-there personality. She decided to blend in with the crowd and see who she might meet.

"Sit, Mariner!" she commanded the dog, leaving him in an area where several other animals shared community water bowls.

Laila headed for the bar and a much-welcome glass of wine. She was sipping on red wine and scoping out the crowd when the man next to her struck up a conversation.

"You must be an artist," he said, eyeing her with a wide smile.

"What would make you think that?"

"Isn't almost everyone on Whidbey? Besides, you just have the look."

Interesting line, but he seemed harmless enough.

"I don't know whether or not everyone on Whidbey is, but if you consider being a copywriter an artistic career, then I guess I am. I'm new to town, by the way."

"Yes, I thought so. You'd be hard to miss otherwise. I'm Con Austin."

Laila flashed him a smile. He was a little offbeat but she liked him.

"And what does Con do?"

"Write poetry. Raise horses. Drink too much when he's bored."

"I'm Laila Stewart. Should I be looking for any of your work in the stores?"

"You can if you're so inclined." Con took a long pull on his beer. "So tell me about this copywriting of yours."

"I write eye-catching advertisements, promotional materials, blurbs for book covers, that kind of thing. Perhaps you'll hire me to do one of your covers," she flirted.

"Sweet. Sounds interesting and fun. Of course I'd hire you."

"Laila." Dara's voice came from someplace behind her. "I see you've met our resident con artist. Don't believe a word he says. He's got an eye for pretty women."

Dara and Con exchanged kisses before Dara linked an arm through Laila's. "If you want to meet some of the people in your business they're in a huddle over there."

Dara twirled her fingers in Con's direction and dragged Laila off to meet the group. Laila was soon involved in a lively debate on the pros and cons of freelancing as opposed to working for a corporation.

The men were attractive in a clean outdoorsy way and far less pretentious than the ones in Florida. But as the evening progressed, Laila found herself missing Hudson. She kept dwelling on the kiss they'd shared.

Periodically she reminded herself of how he'd treated her. It was probably better all around to just move on and forget about him. Hudson was not interested in a real relationship. He wanted a woman he could keep at arm's length and one willing to take a backseat to his business.

Interestingly enough, when they'd first met, Laila had liked it that way. She'd been focused on keeping her business up and running, and having a long-distance friendship worked for her. However, as the relationship developed, she'd found that she wanted to spend more and more time with Hudson. Now she was at a completely different place in her life, she wanted someone willing and able to make a commitment.

She wanted an involvement that would lead to something, although not just with anyone. He had to be a confident man who understood her career was equal to his, who wouldn't feel threatened by her success.

Over time Laila had come to realize that having balance in her life was just as important as making money. Work couldn't be the beginning and end of it all. You needed someone to share the good times and bad with, someone to be your rock.

Con had somehow managed to wiggle his way over. He was engrossed in conversation with one of the more vocal copywriters. After another exchange, peppered with frequent laughter, he wriggled into a spot beside Laila.

"Our celebrity poet and playwright is here," a woman she'd been talking to announced. "Is it true you're being interviewed by Larry King, the on-air personality? Will you be plugging your latest book?"

"Every chance I get."

More laughter followed.

Laila looked at Con with renewed interest. Clearly he wasn't a struggling poet with only two red cents to rub together. There'd been mention of raising horses, and not any old hack got interviewed by King. Con Austin, despite the casual clothing, was somebody.

Con placed an arm around Laila's shoulders.

"Isn't she adorable," he announced to no one in particular. "How's your drink holding up?"

Laila handed him her empty wineglass and he wandered off to the bar.

"Con's something of a player," the same woman who'd called him a celebrity warned. "Guard your heart or he'll break it into little pieces."

There was no danger of her losing her heart to anyone. It had already been shattered. She wasn't about to piece it together and give it to another commitmentphobe.

She was here in Washington because she needed a change of scenery and closure on a romance gone sour.

Con Austin was definitely not about to get what was left of her heart.

Chapter 8

Hudson hung up the phone wondering what it was that his client Talia Chisolm really wanted. The woman had taken to calling him several times a day to grouse about what a bastard her soon-to-be ex was. Although several offers had been put on the table, all of them rather generous as far as Hudson was concerned, Talia turned down each and every one. She always countered with something totally outrageous.

Her latest beef was over silverware that had been in her husband, Brandon's, family for years. Talia wanted every last knife, fork and spoon. Her delaying tactics were racking up quite the bill. She seemed to really want to go to court and play on a jury's sympathy. Since she was the mother of Brandon's two children, and he was the one who'd walked out, the judge would be sympathetic to her cause, or so she thought.

So far, Hudson had only seen a very small percentage of his legal fee. He made a mental note to send Talia another updated invoice. Every spare dime and some was being invested in the winery, and he anticipated that in the next couple of months the business's expenses would escalate. There was pitiful little money coming in.

On top of all that, construction was scheduled to start on the tasting room this week. He and Jon hoped to have the room completed by the time Passport to Woodinville rolled around. The event was a major fund-raiser and attracted an upwardly mobile crowd, mostly from Seattle. Currently there were about thirty wineries participating. The response in previous years had been huge, so passports were limited to the first thirty-five hundred people signing up.

It was the perfect opportunity to showcase Jon Hudson Cellars and provide samples from the first crush. The publicity generated by such an event could very well put Jon Hudson Cellars on the map. Word of mouth was powerful.

Meanwhile to keep the winery open he had to continue working on the career that paid the bills. Three days a week was devoted to their legal practice. He and Jon switched off and on so that there was always one of the owners at the winery.

Hudson even converted one of the rooms in an outer building into law offices for Godfrey Woods, which was what his and Jon's practice was named. Hudson's attention now returned to the folder he'd been examining, as he familiarized himself with the upcoming case. The client's wife had illegally taken their child out of state, ignoring a court order. The desperate father had retained Hudson's services so that he could continue to build a relationship with his daughter.

The jingling phone made him break off from what he was doing. Hudson groaned. Jessica, who normally answered the phones, was off today.

"Law offices of Godfrey Woods."

"I need you over at the main building right away," Jon said, sounding as if he was barely holding on to his sanity. "We've got problems."

Hudson pinched the skin between his eyebrows. What now? he wondered.

"Hudson, are you there?" Jon asked when he still hadn't responded.

"Yes, I'm on my way."

He snapped the folder shut, straightened his shoulders and headed out, preparing for anything. By the time he made it to the main building, it looked like all hell had broken loose. People were scurrying around talking in high-pitched tones.

"What's going on?" Hudson asked, barging into Jon's office and interrupting a meeting.

Scott and Jon, engaged in hushed conversation, looked up.

"We're still reeling from the shock," Jon said.

"Shock?"

"Yes. We had a surprise visit by a sanitation inspector."

"And?"

Hudson narrowed his eyes, waiting. He already suspected he wasn't going to like what he was about to hear.

"And we failed inspection," Jon confirmed.

Hudson came damn close to losing it. It took a lot not to explode.

"How is that possible?"

Shaking his head, Scott Wilkinson looked away before saying, "The inspector thought the wash tube heads inserted into the wine barrels weren't clean enough. If that wasn't bad enough a couple of rodents came out of hiding."

"Rodents, as in rats?"

"Field mice, actually."

"In all my time here I've never seen a mouse in any of these buildings. Not even a dropping. We've always kept things spotlessly clean," Hudson barked.

Scott Wilkinson had gone beet-red.

"The guy that was assigned to clean the equipment's no longer here. I replaced him with an entire team but it looks like something fell through the cracks. I'll take full responsibility and make sure it gets done."

"Did we get a fine?" Hudson probed, and held his breath. He was thinking more money to pay out. More money he didn't have.

"No, luckily just a warning. The inspector gave us a break. He gave us a week to get everything up to code before he returns."

"Let's make sure we pass with flying colors then," Hudson said, stomping out of Jon's office. This was another headache he didn't need. The negative press about poor sanitation could bury them.

Hudson almost missed hearing Laila's greeting.

"Hi, Hudson," she called when he strode past her open door.

"Hey, how's it going?"

"You sound pissed."

Hudson had almost forgotten she'd been scheduled to come in today. The ever-faithful Mariner lay at her feet. There was barely enough space for them in the small cubbyhole.

When the dog woofed a greeting, Hudson bent over to scratch him.

"Hey, Champ, you look relaxed. Do you have everything you need?" he said to Laila.

"Yes, Jon's taking good care of me. I didn't think

you were coming in today. He said you were in court."

Hudson rotated his neck and squared his shoulders.

"The hearing got rescheduled, and a good thing, too. We have some issues that need to be taken care of immediately or we could be out of business. In the four years since I've owned this winery I've never had an animal or bug in any of my buildings, except for the occasional dog." He smiled tightly at Mariner. "Now an inspector happens to come by, and mice come crawling out to greet him."

"What bad timing. Oh, Hudson, I'm sorry."

"Not sorrier than I am. We now have a written warning for unsanitary conditions and a limited time to get the issues rectified. I wonder when this cycle of bad luck will end."

"Oh, come on, try not to be so negative," Laila said, flashing him a teasing smile. "Bad luck comes in threes. You've already had one man hurt, a minor labor uprising and rodents crawling out from some unknown place. Things can only get better. Why don't I show you what I'm working on? Maybe my designs will help cheer you up."

Laila waved to him to come closer. Mariner shifted his position, making space for Hudson.

The moment he got closer Hudson knew it was a huge mistake. He was acutely aware of the clean, fresh, vanilla scent Laila put off. She'd swept all that uncontrollable naturally curly hair off her face with her headband, and all he could see were those prominent cheekbones and her compelling golden eyes. He longed to wind the wiry strands of hair around his fingers and get lost in all that vanilla.

Hudson cautioned himself not to get caught up in emotion again. Being around Laila tested his self-control. It was all about discipline and focus. He needed to be worthy of her before moving forward.

Unfortunately he made the mistake of glancing at her again. Laila was that rare breed of woman who didn't need makeup to enhance her. She had full lips that tilted up at the corners, and right now they were tinged a tempting russet shade. Her long, spiky lashes swept her cheeks as she pointed to the graphics on screen.

"So what do you think? Was this what you had in mind? Did I nail it?"

Hudson used her question as an excuse to hang over her shoulder. With a practiced eye he examined the labels she'd created. Jon would have to agree, as well, and whatever they chose would have to be submitted for approval.

The designs were simple. Instead of the usual mansion in the background or tempting bunch of grapes, a wineglass was the main focus. The words Jon Hudson Cellars were written in various fonts and colors.

"Try changing the color of the border," Hudson suggested. "Make it more of a contrast, and the wineglass will stand out."

With a click of the mouse, Laila complied. She tried several contrasting colors and they narrowed it down to two or three choices to show Jon.

"What about the font? Try making it more legible," Hudson urged. He was still hanging over Laila's shoulder, losing himself in all of her sexy vanilla scent. It took everything he had not to turn her toward him and kiss her until her lips ached.

"No problem."

Laila toggled back and forth trying several fonts, the bracelet's charms jingling with every movement of her hand. Hudson had always found the discreet tattoo on her wrist a turn-on.

He'd enjoyed buying those charms for her. They'd been his way of acknowledging the milestones in her life. He'd always been much better at demonstrating his affection than vocalizing his intentions.

It came from growing up with a father who'd learned to suppress his emotions and hurt. Hudson's father had been devastated when his wife left him. Yet he never spoke of it. When questioned he would only say, "she must have had her reasons."

Consequently, Hudson had learned from an early age not to get too attached to anyone. He'd tried marriage briefly to someone he'd met in law school. That had been a disaster. They were virtual strangers, never establishing any real connection. A year and a half later they were divorced. After that he'd placed a lock around his heart. Then along came Laila, expressive and open. She'd taught him how to feel again.

"If you need to take a break I'll show you my house," Hudson said impulsively.

"You've spoken of it so often I feel like I've already seen it. How about you give me the grand tour at the end of the day?"

"It's in walking distance," Hudson said. "We'll have a meeting and decide on that label."

"Sounds like a plan." Laila shot him a smile that went straight to his heart. She reached down and tickled her dog's neck. Mariner rolled onto his back, sticking all fours in the air. "It was nice of you to let me bring my beast to work with me," she said.

"Wasn't that a condition of your employment?" Hudson joked. "Let me take care of a couple of things and then I'll come get you and we'll head over to the house."

Anticipation made him tackle the mundane aspects of his business with renewed vigor. Laila had brought joy to his life in so many ways. He was beginning to regret breaking up with her, but he'd thought it unfair to string her along when he had no plans to fully commit anytime soon. Right now his energies needed to be focused on business rather than a relationship. There was way too much invested to simply walk away.

For the remainder of the afternoon Hudson made phone calls and tried straightening out his files. When Jon stuck his head in the doorway it was going on five.

"Ready to chuck it in?" he asked. "Laila mentioned something about a meeting at your house after work."

"Yes, I figured we'd have fewer distractions. Any updates on our sanitation problem?"

"Scott's handling it. The exterminator's already been in."

"And the wine barrels are being sanitized?"

"Yes, the heads and hoses were dismantled and cleaned. Luckily there were only a few barrels affected so it's not a huge loss."

"Don't you think it strange that all of a sudden an inspector shows up on our premises to look at tubes and heads, and mice come out of nowhere?" Hudson said out loud, his mind racing.

"I think someone called the Department of Agriculture on us," Jon said, somberly.

"I can't imagine who would do that."

"It might be one or several of the men we refused to take back."

When things hadn't worked out at their new place of business, several of the laborers had returned to the winery asking for their jobs back. Scott had refused to rehire them. He felt not taking them back sent a powerful message.

"I hate to admit it but it sure looks like someone is trying to sabotage us," Jon said as they headed off to get Laila.

The conversation was temporarily put on hold when they arrived at her cubbyhole.

"Ready?" Hudson asked, sticking his head into the small opening.

"Ready. Let me just get a couple of items off the printer and we're on our way."

Laila lined up the papers, placed them in a folder and shoved them into the satchel slung over her shoulder, before following the men.

When Hudson cut through the parking lot and started across the field, Mariner raced ahead of them, stopping to sniff at every bush and mark it as his own.

Hudson had bought the Victorian as a fixer-upper when the elderly owner went to live with his daughter. The proximity to the winery was of course the deciding factor.

The old house had a wraparound porch, wooden floors and way too much space for a bachelor. The bathrooms needed remodeling and the plumbing was faulty, but the home had charm and the workmanship could not be beat. Hudson had fallen in love with the accompanying property with its huge old oak trees and a winding pathway that led to a pond. Fixed up it would be the perfect place to raise kids, but children weren't part of the plan right now.

His guests followed him up an incline toward the side door. The exterior of the building could use a coat of paint but all in good time. They entered a good-size kitchen with wallpaper from another era. That wallpaper would definitely have to go when he had time.

"I've got beer in the refrigerator," Hudson announced. "Wine is of course a staple. If you want anything stronger, the liquor cabinet in the dining room is full."

"I'd like coffee if you have it," Laila asked. "I'll even make it. What about you, Jon?"

"Coffee works fine for me. That was a brisk walk."

Hudson got out the fixings for coffee while Laila pressed her nose against the leaded windowpanes that gave a good view of the back of the property.

"I don't have much to nibble on," Hudson told them. "I haven't had time to go grocery shopping." Needing the connection, he came up behind her and squeezed her shoulder.

Laila turned to face him. "I wasn't expecting you to feed me. I'm going home soon."

"I'll make coffee," Jon hastily offered as if he expected her to run out the front door. "You show Laila around."

Jon must have picked up on the sexual tension between them.

Hudson took Laila's elbow and propelled her along. Mariner kept a sharp eye on them as they began the tour that started in the laundry room. After a quick stop in the dining area Laila was whisked through a formal living room that badly needed updating. They entered an archway leading into a library. A powder room was off to the side and an atrium held a few struggling plants.

All of the rooms had personality but would benefit from some sprucing up. Time and money permitting, the place would be a showpiece. Hudson's plans were to restore the house to its original grandeur. What had sold him on the house was its spaciousness. It was way too much house for him, but it had been priced right, and bargains were few and far between in Washington State.

"Want to see the second floor?" he asked, guiding Laila up a staircase with the kind of banister that he would have enjoyed sliding down when he was young, except there'd been no banister where he grew up. He'd been lucky to have a roof over his head.

Upstairs held four bedrooms, each with its own bathroom. At the end of a hall there was a small alcove he'd converted into a study.

"I love it," Laila commented, pointing out the crown moldings on the ceiling. "The workmanship today is nothing like this."

Hudson had chosen not to invite Laila to his home before because he'd been ashamed. He knew it needed some TLC and updating. He'd been embarrassed to have her stay at the house in its present condition.

"I'd like to see the gardens," Laila said, her hand circling the knob of the French doors leading outside.

Hudson followed her out. "Not much to see this time of year. Everything starts blooming in May and then it's breathtaking."

They started down to the pond where a fine mist hovered over the murky water making it look like a witch's brew.

"Brrr, it's cold."

"I'll warm you up."

Hudson used that excuse as an opportunity to place his arms around Laila's shoulder. As they circled back, Hudson pointed out his efforts at carpentry. He'd built the seating around the towering oaks.

The old magic was still there between them. How could he not touch her or kiss her? She was impossible to resist. Hudson dipped his head and brushed her lips. He got a whiff of that incredible, heady, vanilla smell. Laila tasted even better than she smelled. Her hands pressed against his chest, putting space between them.

"Hudson?" she said breathlessly, her palms splayed across the breadth of him.

He cleared his throat and struggled to bring himself back in check. “I shouldn’t have done that. I apologize.”

She must think he was one confused man. He was confused. It wasn’t such a good idea having her come to the winery after all. He’d have to talk to Jon and put a stop to it. Two to three days of seeing Laila would be agony.

The temptation to hold her in his arms and kiss her senseless would be too much.

Laila Stewart threatened his sanity. And that was exactly why he’d ended it.

Chapter 9

By the time Laila and Hudson returned to the house coffee was waiting. They gratefully accepted the cups Jon handed them.

"You two look frozen," he commented.

Laila wrapped her palms around the warm mug, relishing the heat. "I'm so cold I can't think straight."

Her teeth chattered slightly but she still felt all warm and tingly inside. Hudson's kiss had her blood pumping and her head in an uproar. Starting from today she needed to set some boundaries between them.

Jon's expression remained neutral. It was hard

to guess if he suspected what had actually happened. If so he was smart enough not to let on.

"I'm dying to see what you've been working on all day," Jon said, holding out a chair for Laila and waiting until she was seated.

She searched through her satchel, found the stack of papers and lined them up on the dining room table.

"Here's the rough draft for the Passport to Woodinville copy," she said. "And here are some designs for the wine labels. I also brought a sample of what I think the newsletter should look like. It's all about name and brand recognition. At first glance you should immediately realize you're looking at communication from Jon Hudson Cellars. I took the liberty of picking out your colors."

"Let's see what you came up with," Hudson said, already sifting through the stash.

Jon took the seat next to him.

The men hunched over the samples, scrutinizing them carefully. They made suggestions for several changes and Laila took notes, countering with her own ideas. Work had now become a diversion that served to make her forget the intensity of Hudson's kiss.

After about forty minutes she glanced at her watch, surprised at how fast the time had gone.

"I need to go. The next ferry leaves in half an hour. I'll make the changes and get them back to you as quickly as I can. When do you need me to come in again?"

The partners exchanged looks. Hudson was finally forced to speak up.

"Jon will be in touch with you. Won't you, Jon?"

"Yes, I'll let you know something tomorrow."

How convenient of Hudson to pass the buck. Laila put Mariner on his leash and prepared to head out.

"I'll walk you to your car," Hudson offered.

"That's okay, Jon's already offered."

Considering the sexual tension between her and Hudson it was best not to encourage too much one-on-one time.

Hudson's lips were stretched into a tight line as they headed out.

What was with the mixed signals? She was no one's friend with benefits. He'd made his choice and chose building a business over her. He'd made it clear he had no room in his life for her. She wasn't about to be put on standby waiting for him to fit her into his life.

Laila caught the ferry with several minutes to spare. By the time she got to Whidbey Island it was pitch-dark, and navigating the roads was a challenge. The house was freezing and she quickly lit a fire before playing back her messages on the answering machine. One message got her attention. The president of the local copywriters group wanted to know if she could make their next meeting. That must be Dara's doing or how else would he have gotten her number? There was also a message from Con Austin asking her to return his call.

Rather than jump right on it, Laila heated up some leftover chili, sorted through the mail and read the card from her neighbor, Kent. Kent, in his usually irreverent manner, mentioned that Brock Lawrence seemed to be working out well. He was fitting in nicely with their neighbors on the waterfront.

It reminded Laila she'd made very little effort to meet Brock's neighbors. The weather hadn't exactly been conducive to long walks. Still she should do something about meeting people other than Dara, Con, Jon and Hudson.

She decided to return Con's call before it got too late. Sounding somewhat distracted he answered on the second ring.

"It's Laila Stewart," she said quickly. "Is this a good time for you?"

"How are you, Laila? You caught me in the middle of writing, but that's okay. I really enjoyed speaking with you the other day."

"Me, too."

"Do you like walking?"

She wondered what that was about?

"That depends on the destination."

Con's chuckle was deep and seductive.

"Wherever you want it to be. What I meant to say is that I walk three miles a day and could use a partner. I'm usually up at six and out the door fifteen minutes later. Can I swing by and get you?"

Exercise sounded good to her. She certainly could use to burn some calories, and she'd promised to make a concerted effort to meet people. Con, colorful and connected as he was, might be the ideal person to introduce her around.

"I'd love it," Laila agreed. "We can start tomorrow if you'd like."

"Okay, I'll be at your place around six-thirty. You're on Willow Way, aren't you? Give me the house number."

Laila gave it to him and then hung up. She contemplated what to do with the rest of her evening. She could work on copy, she supposed, but after pushing her creativity to the max all day, she was mentally exhausted and needed to come down.

The phone rang again.

"Hey, you," Dara said. "I know it's late notice but I had a friend cancel on me and I have an extra ticket to tonight's performance of *Dream Girls* at the arts center. It's a visiting troupe and they've had wonderful reviews. Want to go? We could have a drink or a late-night snack afterward."

"Sounds like fun. Give me directions."

Dara told her how to get to the location while Laila hurriedly scribbled down directions. She took a quick shower and changed clothes. This was the Pacific Northwest, and no one got overly dressed up to go anywhere. The black slacks and matching sweater she'd chosen would be the height of fashion.

Laila was still not totally comfortable driving in the darkness, so gave herself plenty of time to get to the Whidbey Island Center for the Arts. Her friend was waiting out front when she pulled up.

"Glad you made it. The play starts in about ten minutes. Let's go find our seats," Dara greeted after giving her a quick hug.

An usher led them down an aisle and waited until they were seated. It was an amazingly full house, and soon she was caught up in the costumes and powerful voices of the leads. The actors without exception were a talented bunch.

"That was wonderful," Laila said afterward. "Thanks for inviting me. Makes me wish I was born in another era. Let's go find a place to have drinks and something to munch on?"

"I know a great bar in walking distance."

"Let's do it, then. I'm buying, by the way."

"No, you aren't."

"Yes, I am."

The tavern turned out to be an old Cape Cod with a white picket fence around it. Dara quickly unlatched the gate and led the way into a toasty interior. Several patrons, all of whom seemed to know each other, gathered around a roaring fireplace, drinks in hand. Laila recognized some of the couples who'd attended the play.

When two Queen Anne chairs became available she and Dara made a leap for them.

"Isn't this place great?" her friend said, sinking into the comfortable upholstery.

"Yes, it's like being entertained in someone's home."

Dara flagged down a nearby server to bring them menus. They placed their drink orders and both women passed the time people-watching.

"What do you think of our little island so far?" Dara asked, leaning in.

"It's great."

"You don't miss Florida and the sun?"

Laila shook her head. "Rarely. I love it here. The people are special."

"You know I wondered what really brought you here. I mean, why would you leave Fort Lauderdale in the middle of winter and come to Washington State? My imagination's gone wild thinking maybe you had a breakdown or something."

"What if I told you that sometimes sunshine gets old? I'm from Baltimore originally and so the cold doesn't bother me. In fact I rather like having the change of seasons."

"I suspect there's more to it than you're saying," Dara said sagely.

Laila took a deep breath. She didn't have to go into detail about her personal life.

"When the opportunity presented itself I needed a change of scenery. I was dating a man who lived here. He began acting up and when I had the chance to do a house swap I came to find out what's really going on."

"And what did you find so far?"

Laila waited until the server set down their appletinis and took their food orders before answering.

"That he's busy 24/7 and doesn't have much time for a relationship. On the other hand he doesn't want to let go, either."

"He sounds confused."

"I don't know what he is, but the push and pull makes it hard to move on. And I still work for him. That makes it even more difficult."

"And you still care for him," Dara finished, leaning in even closer and gazing at Laila over the rim of her martini glass. "How did you happen to end up working for him?"

Laila explained that she'd been hired to write copy, and that Jon Hudson had liked her work so much they kept handing her more assignments.

"You're in a tough spot. But there's no shortage of men here if you like the outdoorsy, woodsy kind. If you don't mind duck shoes and flannel shirts, there's plenty to choose from. There are also the techie types. They're nerdy but brilliant and they're paid well."

"What about African-American men? I haven't seen many around."

"There are a few but you'll have to go into Seattle to meet the single ones. On a completely different note, how would you like to come to the symphony next week and hear me play?"

"I'd love it," Laila said enthusiastically. She was already one step ahead, thinking that maybe at the symphony she might meet the cultured, creative types she got along well with.

The server brought their food and another apple-tini, and the conversation shifted to Con Austin. Laila shared with Dara that he'd called asking her to go walking with him.

"What did you say?" Dara asked her eyes wide. "Con's somewhat controversial and a bit of a ladies' man. You might want to think long and hard about accepting his invitation."

"Controversial in what way?"

"He speaks his mind and doesn't suffer fools easily. He's vocal about the issues he believes in. The man's made a fortune from his poems. He's known as a political satirist."

Laila yawned, and covered her mouth. The long day was finally catching up with her. She pushed her plate away.

"I thought most poets and writers weren't exactly rolling in dough."

"This one's not hurting. He raises Thoroughbreds and he owns a house that would knock your socks off."

"Yes, Con did mention something about that. I assumed he'd inherited money."

"Possibly, but he's very well compensated for what he does. He's conquered a niche market and has an amazing number of fans."

Laila fought back another yawn and signaled for the check.

"I better go home. Six-thirty comes around faster than you know it, and I did promise Con to go walking with him."

"How about you follow me? I know these roads inside and out."

Smothering yet another yawn, Laila followed Dara out.

As darkness approached, Jon and Hudson were still huddled over several files as they planned strategy on an upcoming case. The case was to go before a magistrate the following week. They were representing the husband who would do about anything to have custody of his kids. They felt confident they would win this one although typically the woman usually got custody. But the wife's track record was shaky and there were neighbors willing to testify she was a sad excuse for a mother.

The mother was hooked on prescription drugs

and seemed to thrive on the attention of a succession of boyfriends. The neighbors had stepped in to take care of the kids. On more than one occasion she'd left the children at home unsupervised. It was the neighbors who'd pitched in to feed and care for the children. Therefore they had no problem stepping forward to testify she was an unfit mother. Barring no ugly surprises, Hudson and Jon expected to win. Even so it was best to prepare for the unexpected.

Hudson's head was pounding and his vision had long blurred. It had been a tough day so far and he was no longer productive or thinking straight. He rubbed his eyes and yawned.

"I'm sorry I have to call it quits. I'm about to develop a whopper of a headache," he said.

"You and me both. I'm in court tomorrow. I need to get my sleep," Jon answered, his attention still on the file he was perusing. "Sara Morris is on antidepressants and she's drinking." He pointed to a picture of a passed-out Mrs. Morris. "Poor kids. It has to be tough on them."

"'Tough' is an understatement. They're being raised by strangers."

Hudson yawned again, this time he stood and stretched. "We'll reconnect tomorrow after court? I have to go to bed. We'll need to talk about Laila, as well."

"What about Laila?"

"I've been thinking that maybe it's better to have her work from home."

"Why?" Jon's nose was still buried in the file.

"Because we could use the space she's occupying. If we need her she's only a phone call away."

"What's the real problem?" Jon asked in his usual direct manner. He kept one eye on the file. "Laila's sitting in a converted supply closet for cripe's sake, not some fancy executive suite. What do you need that space for, anyway?"

"I'll think of something," Hudson said, yawning again. "I'm closing shop and heading home."

"Such a wuss," Jon mumbled. "Rather than dealing with your feelings head-on, you'd rather withdraw."

Hudson threw his hands in the air. "Okay, maybe you're right. I find the woman distracting. We have a lot to do in the next three months and I can't afford distractions."

"Was it my imagination? Weren't you two steaming up the room earlier this evening?"

"No, we were not. Just because we're no longer dating doesn't mean I don't enjoy her company."

"Is that what you call it?"

Jon's head was again buried in the file.

"You need to go home," Hudson huffed. "You have a mighty strong imagination. It's not like you're dating up a storm. I don't recall the last time you were out with a woman."

"I was out with Laila on Valentine's night," Jon reminded him. "She is very much a woman."

"Don't remind me."

Hudson wanted to deck him.

"Face it, bro," Jon said. "You don't want Laila, but at the same time you don't want anyone else to have her."

"That's ridiculous," Hudson gritted out, though deep inside he knew there was a kernel of truth to Jon's words.

"Okay, then you won't mind if I show her Seattle and the surrounding areas."

Hudson minded very much but he wasn't about to tell Jon that. It would be playing right into his partner's hands.

"Do what you feel is best. I did offer to play tour guide."

"Did Laila take you up on your offer?"

"Sort of."

"What does 'sort of' mean?"

A banging on the door interrupted the men.

Jon set down the folder. "What the hell. Are you expecting someone?" He headed for the door.

The man on the other side was a stranger.

"Fire," he said. "Your shrubbery went up in flames as I was walking by. The ground under it lit up like a firecracker. I've already called the fire-fighters, but then I saw your light on so I figured you needed to know. It is your property, right?"

"Fire? Where?" Jon asked, already racing off, Hudson behind him.

"Come and I'll show you."

Chapter 10

Laila's Blog
Thursday, March 1

I must be losing my mind. When the alarm went off this morning my head felt like a freight train was roaring through it. I should never have had that second appletini.

After practically sticking my whole head under the faucet I felt much better. At least I could see to find my sweats, and my limbs began to cooperate after that. A glance in the mirror made me realize I was having one of the worst hair days of my life.

I did what any smart woman would do—stuff the entire nappy mess under a cap.

Then I gulped instant coffee and let Mariner out the back door to do his business. My dog looked at me as if I was out of my mind. He gave me one of those looks that said, "Woman, are you crazy? You never get up at this hour."

He was so right. The only time I ever rolled out of bed at an ungodly hour was if I was on a tight deadline for a client, and even then I'd much rather stay up late than get up at the crack of dawn.

I cast another bleary eye in the mirror and damn near died. I am one scary-looking critter at this hour. My front doorbell rang.

Back at you later, after my walk with Con.

"Ready?" Con Austin asked when Laila opened the door. He held a flashlight behind his back, and the rays illuminated the walkway.

"Ready as I'll ever be," Laila grumbled, closing the door behind her and tucking the key and her cell phone deep into the pocket of her sweatshirt.

"Not a morning person, I take it?"

Laila muttered something unintelligible. She was still regretting having that second appletini. Maybe the fresh air would help.

Con wrapped her palm around a steaming cup of coffee. For a brief moment she thought she might retch, but then she inhaled the potent brew and her head slowly began to clear.

"Take a slow sip," Con ordered. "Caffeine eventually helps."

They continued to walk in silence, Con holding the flashlight to light their way.

"Have you gotten a lot of copywriting business since you've been here?" he asked.

"I have a client in Woodinville, but most of my clients are in other states. Thankfully, I don't need to go into an office to deliver."

"You might want to consider doing work for the Whidbey Island Chamber of Commerce," Con suggested. "We're a vacation destination and each town has its own commerce. There are Web sites and visitors' guides that could benefit from the help of a professional copywriter. I know I could certainly use your help."

"How so?" Laila asked, her curiosity piqued.

"I have three books of poetry being released in the next year or two. I could use your help with cover design and back blurbs. Do you have experience in that area?"

"Actually I do have some."

Con picked up the pace, swinging his arms, ramping up their walk a notch. "Writing cover copy might be something to specialize in. Usually publishers hire freelancers. You could go off in a whole other direction."

"Sounds like something to think about. You have

that much clout with your publishing house? They'd hire who you suggested?"

"Let's just say I get what I want."

Dara had mentioned that he was something of a maverick. In reality they weren't that different. Laila had always colored outside of the lines.

"I own my publishing house," Con explained. "I wouldn't mind seeing samples of your work, though. I've been looking for a good copywriter for quite some time."

It was a wonderful opportunity, but right now her first priority lay with Jon Hudson Cellars. She had a relatively small window of time to produce the work they'd contracted her for and, as much as she welcomed a challenge, she couldn't see herself taking on any new assignments right now.

"I have quite a number of projects that I'll need to deliver in the next month or so, but I'll be happy to e-mail you samples of my copy and share with you my client list," she said.

"Do that," Con encouraged as they started up an incline that would definitely test how fit she was.

Laila managed to huff and puff her way to the top. She was certainly getting a workout, and it made her realize that not going to the gym, as she had been doing in Fort Lauderdale, was not necessarily a good thing.

A hint of daylight broke through the grayness of

the morning. Con aimed his flashlight on the pedometer he carried.

"Another one and a half miles to go," he announced.

"Hopefully not uphill."

"Some of it uphill. We'll have breakfast and then walk back."

They continued on for another twenty minutes and then slowed down in front of Chow Down, where she'd first met Dara.

Even at that hour, the café held a good-size crowd. Judging from their flushed appearances several had been jogging and stopped by for a quick caffeine fix. A few had their heads buried in a newspaper. Laila couldn't wait to sit down. She was thirsty and winded, and a cool liquid sounded good to her.

Con quickly found them seats and immediately ordered bottled water. As they sipped from their respective bottles, he handed her a menu.

"What looks good to you?" he asked, scanning his own menu.

"I'm going with the bagel and cream cheese." She closed her menu and set it down.

The cell phone in her pocket vibrated, causing her to squirm.

"Something the matter?" Con asked.

Laila retrieved the phone and glanced at the window.

"I'll need to take this," she said, rising and stepping away. She placed a finger in one ear so she could hear better.

"Good morning!"

"Laila, I'm sorry to call so early."

The warm timbre of Hudson's voice brought her immediately on the alert. She squelched the tingly feeling that started at the base of her gut and worked its way up.

"Did you need me to come in?" she asked, wondering what had prompted him to call.

"Can you? There was a fire last evening, and things are in turmoil. Jon has to be in court and my admin seems to have deserted me. The media's gotten wind of things and phones are ringing off the hook. Scott Wilkinson, our manager, is in but there's only so much he can do. We really need someone with a good head on their shoulders to answer phones and hold down the fort. Please, I can use your help. You'll be well compensated, I promise."

She should be flattered that Hudson had reached out to her, even trusted her enough to ask for her help. She knew how much he'd invested financially and emotionally in the winery. Because of what they'd shared, she couldn't let him down.

"If you can give me a couple of hours I'll be there," Laila said, her mind mentally racing. A fire was disastrous and the last thing Hudson needed right now. When would his streak of bad luck end?

"Bless you," he said. "And, Laila, be sure to bring Mariner with you and a change of clothing. It's going to be a long day and you might want to consider spending the night."

Spending the night in close proximity to him?

Laila returned to the table to find Con engaged in conversation with a woman she'd never met. She nodded her hello.

"Excuse me, something's come up and I'm going to have to leave. I'm sorry."

Con's forehead wrinkled. "That's awfully sudden."

"A client is having a crisis. I'm going to get a taxi and head back."

"Have Marilyn call you a taxi," the woman talking to Con said, jutting a thumb at the interior of the café. "She's the owner."

"I'll speak to Marilyn," Con offered, loping off in the direction of the owner.

"How long have you known Con?" his companion asked, once he was out of earshot. "I'm Francine, by the way."

"I'm Laila. I just moved here from Fort Lauderdale. I've only known Con for a short time."

"Be careful. He's not the committed type."

Laila wisely did not comment. She excused herself when she could, and hurried toward the exit in time to see a car with the sign Whidbey Island Taxi pull up. Con saw her into the cab, and she promised to be in touch when she returned from Woodinville.

Back at the carriage house Laila took a quick shower and stuffed a few personal items and a change of clothing into a backpack. She glanced at the ferry schedule and called for Mariner, who was outside doing his business.

In less than an hour the ferry docked in Mukilteo and she was on the highway heading for Woodinville. As she approached the wrought-iron gates of the vineyard she noticed several vans parked out front. Men and women milled around, some speaking into cell phones. These were paparazzi, she assumed, like vultures descending at the first hint of news.

Laila drove her car through the open gates and toward the main building. So far she'd not seen one visible piece of evidence that there had been a fire. She entered the Victorian house to find people she didn't know jabbering at a rapid pace into whatever telephones they could find. Hudson held two phones to his ears, juggling them adeptly. He was speaking into his cell phone while the office phone dangled from a cord in his other hand.

Spotting her, his eyes lit up.

"Hang on just a sec," he said to the person on the other end of his cell. "Hey, Laila, can you handle this, please?" He thrust the landline at her.

She had just enough time to toss her purse on the desk and take Mariner off his leash. She waited for the dog to sit, thinking it was a good thing she'd brought the overnight bag she'd left in the car.

"Jon Hudson Cellars," she said into the mouthpiece. "What can I help you with?"

"Is the owner there?" a female voice asked.

"What's this in reference to?"

The woman explained she was calling from a staffing agency, hoping to place a number of workers with the vineyard.

"We'll need to get back to you. Give me your number," Laila said.

The moment she hung up, the phone rang again. She would have to wing it. Hudson still had his cell phone glued to his ear. Laila got the impression from the bits and pieces floating her way that Jon was filling him in on the case he was representing. Gathering she was on her own she picked up the ringing phone.

"Jon Hudson Cellars."

"Hi, Roberta Sullivan from King Television. Are you in a position to answer questions about last night's fire?"

"No, I'm not," Laila said, keeping it brief.

"Then who is?"

"A representative from our PR department should be able to help you, but no one's available right now. I can have someone get back to you if you'd like."

Why hadn't Hudson considered having a written

statement prepared? It would have helped immensely and there would be no winging it.

"I'd rather speak to someone now," the reporter insisted.

"The winery will be releasing a formal statement shortly," Laila fibbed.

She tried to get Hudson's attention but he was still absorbed in his conversation. The moment she put the receiver down the phone rang again. Such madness. Who would ever have thought that a fire on the grounds would generate this much interest?

"Jon Hudson Cellars," she greeted. "Are you able to hold for a moment?"

When the caller said she could, Laila waved a hand at Hudson who had ended his conversation. She stabbed at a button placing the person on hold.

"Would you like me to draft a standardized response so that everyone answering the phones says the same thing?" she asked.

"Go ahead if you think it would help." Hudson sounded frazzled and not at all like himself. "Just make sure I see it before it goes public."

"I will."

Carrying his cell with him Hudson wandered off outside. Laila took a brief respite to draft a response to the questions that were being flung at them. She found Hudson, who scanned the wording and gave his nod. Laila then printed out several copies and handed it to everyone on the phones;

people she had yet to officially be introduced to. For the next several hours she took calls and did whatever needed doing.

At some point Hudson must have requested additional security because soon a group of muscle-bound men were patrolling the property and things seemed more in control. Even so, by the end of the day Laila was fried.

She felt as if she'd been a one-person call center, although the truth was that there'd been several people on the phones. There'd been no time to do what Jon Hudson Cellars was really paying her for—write copy. But the smoldering looks that Hudson kept tossing her way more than made up for the inconvenience of being stuck on the phones. At least he appreciated her help.

Considering all they'd been through, they could still be friends. And maybe it was better this way.

Chapter 11

"You've done enough," Hudson said, coming up to Laila and massaging her aching shoulders. "How about taking a break and allowing me to buy you dinner?"

A tremor started somewhere at the base of her gut but she was not about to let on how much his touch affected her.

"I'd like that," she answered, smiling.

It had been ages since she'd sat across a table from Hudson. And although she'd always enjoyed their time together, this would probably be another painful meander down memory lane. Breaking bread with Hudson tonight would only be two people eating together and not a romantic event.

In the past they'd had some wonderful dinners that had been a prelude to a sexually satisfying evening. Although they'd lived in different states, whenever they'd gotten together they'd always been in sync. Their lovemaking had been intense and passionate. They'd connected and Laila still missed those intimate times together.

She gathered her things and called to Mariner who'd been eyeing the activity around him with some trepidation. He happily bounded over. Hudson, instead of heading for the Infiniti, started across the grounds in the direction of his home.

"I…I th-thought we were going to a restaurant," Laila sputtered, increasing her stride to catch up with him. Having dinner with Hudson at home was asking for trouble. She'd wrapped her head around being just friends, but still… Mariner meanwhile was already racing ahead as if he knew exactly where he was going.

"No, going to a restaurant is much too risky," Hudson said. "Reporters are probably still camped outside of the property and I'm only going to get irritated if they start asking questions. I was thinking maybe we'd just take it easy and order in."

Laila glanced at her watch, mentally calculating how much time before the last ferry to Whidbey left. She still hadn't made up her mind about staying over, and if she did stay, she planned on finding a hotel, which she assumed Hudson would pay for. She was there at his request, after all.

He took the front steps two at a time and stood on the wraparound porch waiting for her to catch up. Laila's treacherous dog sat right beside him, tongue lolling.

Inside, Hudson flipped on the light and waved her into a leather recliner. It was teeth-chattering cold. When he squatted down to light a fire, Laila got a most appealing view of him from the rear. She didn't like where her thoughts were heading.

"Might as well get warm and comfortable," Hudson said. "What do you feel like eating?"

"Thai sounds good to me."

She'd barely gotten the words out before Hudson was on the phone, ordering from a menu that he'd retrieved from the kitchen.

"Is there anything you didn't order?" she joked after he'd completed the call. "You'll have food for weeks."

"It's been a long day. Aren't you starving?"

She was hungry, but there was only so much that anyone could eat. Hudson was bound to have leftovers.

"You could do me a favor while we wait for our food to be delivered," Hudson said, curving a finger at her and beckoning her over.

"I'd be happy to help wherever I can."

"How about sampling Jon Hudson's wines and giving me an honest answer about what you think."

"Bring it on. I can't go overboard, though, just in case I have to drive."

"You're spending the night," Hudson said firmly. "It's been a long day and I may need you to bail me out again tomorrow."

"That's probably wise."

There had to be a nearby motel; someplace that would take a dog if need be. At some point she'd work that into the conversation.

Hudson headed for the kitchen, returning with several unlabeled bottles and clean wineglasses on a tray.

"Most are blends of classic Bordeaux," he announced.

"What's a blend?" Laila hoped her total ignorance didn't show.

"A Bordeaux blend may involve several kinds of grapes. A blended red, for example, would be a combination of two primary grapes, say, a Cabernet Sauvignon and a Merlot. You could also have a Cabernet Franc, a Petit Verdot, a Malbec and a Carménère."

"It's all French to me," Laila quipped, giggling.

Hudson let out a belly roar. "Ready for your taste test, young lady?"

"Sure. I'm no expert but I know what I like." Laila held out one of the empty wineglasses.

"It's all a matter of what appeals to your palate."

Hudson gave her one of his smoldering glances. Laila steeled herself not to get pulled in.

"Here's how it works," he said. "When I pour the red, check to see if the color's maroon, purple, ruby, garnet or brownish. A white should be clear or strawlike, golden, light green, pale yellow or brown in appearance. We'll start with a red."

"What am I looking for?"

"You're checking for the wine's opacity. Is it clear, cloudy, transparent or opaque?"

Dutifully Laila peered down into her glass. "It looks clear to me."

"Good. Now tilt your glass a bit and give it a little swirl. This time you're looking for color, clarity and brilliance. Imagine you're examining a diamond. Is there sediment, cork or any other floating bits? Older red wines tend to be more translucent than younger reds."

Laila was beginning to enjoy this lesson in wine tasting immensely. She was also enjoying Hudson's company, maybe a little too much. Upon occasion their glances locked and held. She was transported back to a time when there had been an unbeatable connection between them, when they didn't need words to communicate.

"Now swirl your wine and take a sniff," Hudson ordered, breaking the spell.

"Why?"

"Because that way you can fully appreciate the aroma. Take a quick whiff and go with your first impression."

Obediently Laila inhaled the burgundy liquid.

"That's one wussy sniff," Hudson joked. "Stick your nose down into that glass and inhale. What are your second impressions now? Is the smell oak, berry, floral, vanilla or citrus? A wine's aroma is an excellent indicator of its quality and unique characteristics. Much like a woman's scent, you can tell a lot by it. Go on, sniff again just to be sure."

She'd been asked to taste test Hudson's wine, and hadn't anticipated it would be such a sensual experience with double entendres filled with hidden meaning being flung around. The scent of a woman was definitely a personal thing.

When she ventured another look at Hudson, his eyes were closed as he savored his wine. Maybe she was making way too much of this intimate experience.

"Taste," Hudson urged. "Start with a small sip and let the liquid roll around your tongue. Taste, relish and enjoy."

Laila stared at his full lips; the way his Adam's apple bobbed up and down as he swallowed the liquid. His pleasure was so apparent. It was as if he were drinking an elixir.

"Now that you have an initial impression, allow

a small breath of air in through your lips, like this," he instructed, demonstrating.

It took all that she had not to fling herself at him. Laila felt the heat start at her toes and work its way up her legs. She attributed the flush spreading through her body to the fire he'd built and the accelerated beat of her heart to exerting herself all day.

"Allow the wine to mingle with the air," Hudson said, again demonstrating. "Like this. It's called swirling. You're able to taste the flavors more fully. What do you taste now, Laila?"

Taste? She could still taste him on her lips from the last time he kissed her.

"I'm not sure. What am I looking for?"

Laila tried to rein in her wayward thoughts and quickly imitated Hudson. She'd privately thought that the people she saw at restaurants making a huge production of tasting wines were poseurs simply out to make an impression. Now she realized that appreciation of good wine was almost an art form.

Hudson's voice came at her soothing and sexy.

"Reds will often have a berry, woody or bell pepper taste. White wines will have an apple, floral or citrus flavor."

She nodded her head thinking that the only flavor that stuck with her now was the remembrance of the taste of his skin; slightly musky but pleasantly so.

"An introduction to a new wine is like your first time meeting a woman," Hudson said in the same sonorous tones. "On the first encounter there's an initial impression. Then there's the finish, the thing you remember last. Does she stick in your mind after that first encounter, or is she simply a distant memory with nothing outstanding to commend her?"

Did she stick in his? Apparently not or he would never have let her go.

Time to move on, she reminded herself for the hundredth time. She'd come to get closure, and in so many ways she had.

Hudson was doing it again, reeling her in, the analogy to a woman both romantic and seductive.

They repeated the tasting process, trying several different blends. As the wine kicked in, Laila was slowly letting her guard down. It was like being with the old Hudson, not the distant stranger he'd become.

"Maybe I'm getting tipsy, but they all taste pretty good to me," she said, clinking her glass against Hudson's. "All of your wines are winners as far as I'm concerned."

He raised his glass and took a sip. "Let's hope the public thinks so, as well."

The doorbell chimed, breaking the electric connection. Hudson went off to answer it, returning with several brown bags in hand.

"We can eat in the kitchen or pretend we're picnicking in front of the fire," he said, with a teasing smile thrown her way.

"I'm up for a picnic. Sitting in front of the fireplace sounds wonderful."

"Then let me grab a tablecloth, some cutlery and napkins, and I'll be back."

"I'll help you."

Laila rose from her chair, her legs wobbling unsteadily. The wine was catching up with her. Luckily the decision to drive or not drive had been taken away from her. She brought the items Hudson handed her back into the living room, spread the cloth in front of the fireplace and set out the tableware.

Mariner lounged in front of the fireplace, an eye open for handouts.

"With a little sprucing up this house could be magnificent," she said, looking around.

"Yes, but it requires time and money. Neither of which I have right now."

"How did the fire get started?" she asked. "You were lucky it didn't spread to the actual building."

"Yes, I know. The fire inspector thinks it might be arson. I prefer to think not."

"Why would someone want to purposely set a fire?" Laila asked, spooning shrimp pad Thai onto her plate and then handing Hudson the carton. She made up a little plate, which Mariner quickly devoured.

"Interestingly enough the fire started in the area where we planned on building that tasting room.

The foundation had just been laid. Thanks to the quick actions of a man walking by, there was minimal damage, but now cleanup is going to set us back several days."

Laila helped herself to a skewer of chicken satay and bit into the succulent meat. "Delicious," she said when she was finally able to speak. "It's almost as if someone's trying to scare you off."

"But who? Most of the wineries around are well established. We're the new kids on the block, totally unproven and so there should be no reason to feel threatened."

"You've made no enemies that you know of?"

"None."

"It's mighty peculiar if you ask me."

Hudson reached over to pour from a bottle he'd just opened.

"Try this Cab and tell me what you think. But before you do let's toast."

Hudson picked up his glass and clinked it against hers.

"To my first crush."

"To your first crush."

She imagined he was referring to wine and not her. No point in reading into his words.

Following his instructions, Laila checked for the wine's opacity. She swirled the liquid, looking for color, clarity and brilliance before taking a sip.

"Mmmmm," she pronounced. "This is a winner as far as I am concerned."

"Yes, it's quite good."

They sampled several more dishes, and by the time the meal ended they'd killed most of the bottle.

Laila was feeling more than a little tipsy by the time she helped Hudson put away the leftovers. They kept reminiscing about shared events and giggling over how silly they'd been.

"How are you doing in general?" Hudson asked, his hand caressing her arm.

"Great. I wanted a change of scenery and it was a good move coming here. I've made friends."

"Male friends?"

What business of it was his?

"Yes, in some cases, men."

She was acutely aware of Hudson's index finger drawing patterns on her flesh. His jaw muscles twitched and his hold on her tightened.

"I never meant to mislead you," he said softly, looking directly into her eyes. Hudson was so close she could smell the wine on his breath. She thought about how he'd described a wine's finish. He was the one who'd lingered in her mind. She was working on making him a distant memory.

The wine made her brave. There were answers she needed so that she could finally put him behind her and move on.

"I guess I'll never understand what happened with us."

"I don't know if I could begin to explain," he said, dipping his head and capturing her lower lip between his teeth and nibbling gently.

She should push him away and take back her power, but his kiss left her breathless. Laila wrapped her arms around his neck and savored the wonderful fruity taste of his tongue.

The room was now unbearably warm. It must have to do with the crackling fire. Thankfully she had Hudson's arms to anchor her.

"You'll stay with me tonight," he said.

Instead of insisting otherwise, she giggled. "I'm much too tipsy to attempt the drive home but maybe I could make it to a hotel."

"Neither of us is in the condition to drive."

"A hotel might have a courtesy van. I'm sure they'll pick up."

"What about Mariner?"

What about him? She'd almost forgotten about her dog pretending to sleep but really eyeing them over his paws.

"There's got to be a place that will take Mariner."

"I'll be happy to take both of you," Hudson said slyly.

Laila giggled nervously. "We don't want to be an imposition."

When Hudson kissed her again, her resolve

crumbled. He wasn't some stranger she'd picked up in a bar. They'd been good together; at least, she'd thought so. Sex between them had never been anything but wonderful.

"I'm getting tired. Let's go to my bedroom and stretch out," he urged. "The house might need updating but the sound system is state-of-the-art, and I still have the best DVD collection around."

"Uh."

Hudson's kiss was the deciding factor. It filled her up and almost made her burst. It was better than any full-bodied red she'd ever tasted. When Hudson wrapped his arms around her, Laila practically floated upstairs. She sat on the king-size bed as he quickly discarded his clothes.

Hudson's body was copper-colored and toned. It reminded her of a trophy that star athletes got for placing in the top three, the kind you displayed in a cabinet and took out to gape at on occasion. If she ever got the chance to take him home again she'd never leave him to get dusty on her shelf.

"Aren't you going to undress?" Hudson asked her.

"I was waiting for you to undress me," she said, waving her wrist of charms at the same time extending the lascivious invitation.

It was all the urging Hudson needed. In a blink of an eye he was on his knees, and had the sweatshirt she'd thrown on that morning over her head.

He tugged on the zipper of her jeans, and Laila quickly wiggled out of the confining material. She was wearing her one feminine indulgence: thong panties and a front-clasp bra purchased at an up-market boutique.

Hudson already had an index finger hooked in the clasp of her bra. She could feel her nipples pebbling.

"I've always liked your taste in undies," he said.

He'd given her lingerie as presents, but not this matching set. She'd bought these with no help from him, wanting to feel sexy again not for a man but for herself.

Laila's full breasts spilled into Hudson's waiting palms. He cupped both of them and used his thumb to stroke her already hardened nipples. It didn't take much to get Laila going. In her excitement she bit his earlobe and that elicited a groan of pleasure.

Hudson buried his nose in her cleavage, moistening the flesh with his tongue. One hand slipped beneath the elastic waistband of her thong, delving into her moist curls. In a few short agonizing seconds he'd found her sweet spot. She was squirming and bucking and holding him in her hands, giving him as good as she got.

Hudson's rough tongue traced a liquid path south. When he got closer to his mark Laila's insides quivered and her entire body pulsed. The drumming at her core became a rapid staccato.

Hudson pressed his lips to her center, ramping up the beat another notch.

Laila thought she would leap out of her skin. She wanted to feel the full length of him inside of her. The things he was doing to her with his tongue should be bottled and sold to the highest bidder.

Hudson pushed her back against the pillows and, using his knee, pried apart her thighs. He left her momentarily to rummage through the nightstand and returned with a small foil package in his hand. Laila helped him sheath himself. She didn't want to ruin the mood and let her imagination run wild wondering why Hudson had condoms in his drawers.

Soon he was nestled between her thighs, and Laila's nails raked his back. Hudson's exits and entries were slow and calculated, making her call out his name. With every bittersweet stroke she came closer to finding release. If only time would stand still. That was wishful thinking on her part. She would do well to savor every last moment.

There was no way they could get back to the level of intimacy that had kept them bonded. There would be no going back.

She and Hudson were at different places in their lives. A sensible woman would be smart to move on.

Was she a sensible woman?

Chapter 12

Hudson stared out the window of his office hoping against all odds that there would be a glimmer of sunlight on the horizon. But the sky up above held only the promise of more gray. Washington State was way overdue for some sun.

Today he was determined to focus his attention on the winery. His employees relied on him to be a role model. If he didn't put on a good face, then the rumor mill would be speculating more than it already did. He needed to squelch those rumors quickly.

Now, more than any other time, it was important to establish himself as a leader. He couldn't expect

Scott Wilkinson, the vineyard manager, to handle all the issues or questions that came up. It was way too much for one person; especially a new person.

Hudson had made the difficult decision to turn over his legal clients to Jon temporarily. Jon was now handling the negotiations associated with Talia Chisolm's divorce. But Talia was not at all pleased that she was handed off to Jon. She'd called several times and left nasty messages. She was expecting Hudson to call her back. He'd do that eventually.

Hudson tried his best to focus. He was still having some difficulty getting his arms around what had transpired between him and Laila last evening. He should have exerted more self-control and not allowed things to get so out of hand. It wasn't as if he was some eighteen-year-old kid with raging hormones.

He focused on the computer monitor and the e-mails coming in. Visions of Laila's naked body and limbs entwined with his were still vivid in his mind. He could still touch her, feel her and taste her. Now he was even more determined to put some distance between them. Somehow he would convince Jon she needed to work from home. Having her around was way too distracting.

Hudson had actually been glad when Laila suggested catching the midday ferry back to Whidbey Island that morning. Judging by the e-mails he'd already received, she was at work. She'd always been disciplined, so there should be no problem with her setting up shop at home.

Although there was little or no awkwardness between them that morning, he was glad for the space. Guilt was now rearing its ugly head. Hopefully he hadn't misled her into believing they would pick up where they left off, because he was in no way ready to commit. Last evening alcohol and a basic primal need had clouded his judgment. Now in the clear light of morning he realized he should never have allowed himself to get carried away.

He couldn't blame it all on alcohol. He'd engineered the way the evening would go. The wine tasting had been an excuse to keep her at his house and try to reconnect. And he'd done it knowing that he was not able to offer her a future; at least not until his business was on more stable ground.

She'd seemed to take it all in stride. At least, she appeared to. She'd sat in for Jessie that morning, answering phones and typing letters. She'd even briefed his assistant when she finally showed up on what had transpired to date. And once things calmed down and the extra security he'd hired showed up, she'd been out there like a shot heading for the ferry.

A knock on Hudson's door brought him back to the business at hand.

Scott Wilkinson stuck his head through the open door.

"Do you have a minute?" he asked.

"Of course. Come in."

Scott entered and took a seat in the chair directly across from him.

"What's up?" Hudson asked.

"The rumor mill is way out of control but I can handle that. Any updates in terms of the fire?"

"Nothing new, actually. I'm expecting to hear something from the fire chief once he speaks with the arson investigator."

"Does seem suspicious, doesn't it?"

"I'd say. Someone's trying to send me a message."

Scott stood, squaring his shoulders. "I should be getting back to work. When you have time I'd like to talk to you about the talk going on about the union's demands to protect their emloyees."

Hudson groaned. "That's just what we need—more union demands."

The intercom on Hudson's desk buzzed. He stabbed a finger at the button.

"What is it, Jessie?"

"It's Talia Chisolm again," Jessie, the student who served as his admin, said.

Hudson huffed out another breath and muttered an oath.

"And on that note, I'm off." Scott Wilkinson ambled toward the door. "I'll try to get on either your calendar or Jon's later this week and I'll fill you in."

"Do that." Hudson's attention returned to Jessie. "Did Ms. Chisolm say what she wanted?"

"Only that it was important that she speak with you."

"Okay, put her through."

Hudson inhaled another calming breath and then slowly exhaled. He wondered what was up with the high-maintenance diva. He'd called her and left a message that Jon would be filling in for him temporarily.

The connection was made and Talia came on the line.

"Hudson, is that you?"

"Yes, Talia? Is something wrong?"

They'd been on first-name basis for a while, only because the soon-to-be-ex-Mrs. Chisolm had insisted on it.

"Why are you throwing me to the wolves?" she demanded.

"Throwing you to the wolves, as in…?"

"Handing me off to an associate."

Hudson pinched the skin between his furrowing brow. "Jon's my partner and he's been briefed on your situation. He's a very competent attorney with an excellent reputation."

"I prefer dealing with you," Talia whined. "We've always had a good rapport."

Hudson decided he might as well lay it on the line with her.

"Another situation has come up that requires my

undivided attention. I'd be shortchanging you if I didn't turn you over to Jon."

"A situation that's more important than I am? I'm not as comfortable with Jon as I'm with you," Talia carped. "How about you and I have dinner and talk about a solution?"

"Unfortunately I don't have the time right now. Jon can make himself available if you'd like."

"I don't want to have dinner with Jon. I want to have dinner with you."

Talia was both persistent and demanding. He'd have to stick to his guns. Luckily Jessie stuck her head in the open door. She held a finger in the air indicating she required his attention.

"The fire chief is on the phone," she mouthed loud enough for him to hear.

"Talia, I have to go. Give Jon a chance. He'll do his best by you and he'll keep me up to speed on any developments."

"But…"

"You're in good hands." Hudson hung up before she could get in another word.

He depressed the lit button Jessie pointed to.

"Hudson Godfrey."

"I just wanted to keep you updated, Mr. Godfrey."

The fire chief gave him the results he'd gotten from the arson inspector. It confirmed what they'd long suspected, that the fire had been intentionally set. A kerosene can had been found in a trash can not too far from the scene. Currently it was being examined for fingerprints.

"One of the detectives will be by shortly to give you all the details," the fire chief said before hanging up.

Hudson had hoped that the result would prove otherwise. He did not want to believe that someone had it in for him. Stepping up security was costing him money the business didn't have. He also wasn't sure whether his insurance policy covered a building that hadn't yet been fully constructed. He made a mental note to have Jessie or Scott call and find out.

More and more he'd begun to think that he needed an office manager to take care of tedious details so that he could concentrate on the winery. But that would mean adding another head to the payroll, and right now that was out of the question.

He had interviews set up today and tomorrow for the tasting-room manager's position. Talk about bad timing. Perhaps he could postpone these interviews until next week.

Hudson thumbed through his day planner but couldn't find when he'd scheduled the first interview.

"Jessie," he called, "what does my calendar look like for the next week?"

A few seconds later Jessie strode in and slapped a sheet of paper on his desk.

"Here it is. By the way, your meeting with the WAWGG is in less than an hour. You'll need to get going."

"Shoot, I forgot I was attending the Washington Association of Wine and Grape Growers gathering. That's one meeting I don't want to miss. It's an excellent networking opportunity."

Jessie pointed to his schedule. "You're interviewing three people tomorrow for the tasting manager's position."

Hudson groaned. "Now I'm not going to have time to supervise the cleanup from the fire. I'd also planned on meeting with the contractor to see when construction can begin again. Get hold of the insurance company today and find out if they've got an update as to whether or not I'm covered for the damage?"

Jessie scribbled a note on the pad she was carrying.

"Got it. Now you better get going if you want to make that meeting."

Hudson was seriously considering changing his mind. Perhaps he needed to stay close to home and not go gallivanting off to some industry meeting. It wasn't as if Jon would be here to cover for him. On the other hand, leaving the premises for a while might be the best thing. It was a tight-knit industry and word about the fire would have gotten out. What better way to hear about the rumors circulating than to chat with his peers, and truthfully he'd had just about enough aggravation for the day.

"Try to reschedule tomorrow's interviews if you can," Hudson said, grabbing the jacket on the back of his chair and slipping into it.

"Sorry, I can't do anything about the first one. She's already at her hotel. She drove in from Walla Walla as you asked her to."

Hudson smothered a loud groan.

"It's probably too late to cancel that one, then. Try not to spend the night, will you? If Jon calls let him know I'll be in touch later."

"Be careful driving," Jessie called after him.

"I will."

He would need all of his concentration to navigate the roads. He'd tried his best to put visions of Laila out of his head all day. Sex had always been good between them, but last night was way off the chain, surpassing anything he'd ever experienced. He'd lost himself in her edible vanilla smell.

It couldn't happen again. He wouldn't let it. He wasn't being fair to her and he didn't want to string her along. He'd never planned on getting this attached. And emotionally attached, he was.

Laila made herself focus. She'd been chastising herself all day for being weak. She should never have slept with Hudson again. Instead of getting over him and moving on, she was back right where she'd started.

Ever since returning from the winery, she'd tried her best to put last night behind her. She'd thrown herself into perfecting the flyers for Passport to Woodinville. The mailing was to be targeted to a select group of wine lovers. It would be a special invitation requesting guests put Jon Hudson Cellars on their preferred list of places to visit. In return every patron passing through Jon Hudson's wrought-iron gates would be given a wineglass.

Laila focused on her monitor again, rereading the words she'd typed and silently congratulating herself. It was probably some of the best copy she'd written since coming to Washington State.

With Passport to Woodinville only a few weeks away, an event historically well attended, the public interest would be piqued. This could be make-it-or-break-it time. The copy she was writing needed to be so dynamic it would pull in people.

Laila attributed her most recent creative spurt to last evening's events. She'd fantasized about last night throughout the entire process. Hudson had been foremost in her mind as she'd typed away. She'd envisioned the muscles and sinew of Hudson's nude body. When she closed her eyes briefly, she could still feel his hands on her flesh, probing her in the most intimate of places.

That heavenly musky smell that was uniquely Hudson's still lingered in her nostrils. It proved to be far more intoxicating than any Merlot, Shiraz or

Cabernet. Hudson Godfrey was his own unique vintage.

Laila read out loud what she'd just written.

"Wine with Jon Hudson! We listen!"

A play on words and both innovative and eye-catching, at least so she thought. People should get it. Why was she second-guessing herself? Jon and Hudson had been pleased with the five-percent response rate on a twenty-thousand mailing. That wasn't half-bad especially since a good response rate was considered to be two to three percent.

When her phone rang, Laila was almost reluctant to answer it. But what if it was Hudson? She could hope, couldn't she? She tore her eyes away from the monitor and went off to answer. The voice on the other end wasn't the one she'd expected. She tamped down on her disappointment.

"Con Austin here. I showed up for our walk this morning but you weren't there." He sounded annoyed and she couldn't blame him. She'd forgotten all about Con.

"I'm so sorry," Laila said, forcing her voice to be lively. "I spent the night in Woodinville. My client had an emergency and so I stayed to help out. I should have called and canceled, but with everything going on, our walking engagement went clear out of my head."

Con chuckled. "Would that be the client friend you went scurrying off to help? I must have made quite the impression, huh? Out of sight, out of mind. You can make it up to me this weekend by attending my poetry reading if you'd like. Of course, I'll be expecting you to play the role of groupie."

Laila liked that he had a sense of humor.

"That's very tempting. Can I get back to you?" she said.

"Are you blowing me off?"

"Not at all. I promised my client to remain available in the event he needed additional help."

It was a little white lie but at least it bought her time. She was honest enough to acknowledge that her emotions were on a wild roller-coaster ride right now. She didn't want to mislead Con or let him think that she was ready to get involved. He might not be looking for a serious relationship, but she wasn't about to be a convenient hookup, either. She'd learned her lesson.

"I'll see you tomorrow for our walk, then. Call me if something changes."

Laila thought about Con Austin for all of two seconds after she hung up. He was a colorful character but didn't hold a candle to Hudson. Was she letting lust and familiarity cloud her judgment?

On second thought maybe she really should give Con a chance. She had the feeling it would be more of the same with Hudson.

Chapter 13

Laila's Blog
Wednesday, March 14

I've been trying my best to forget about Hudson but all I keep thinking about is how good we were in bed together. We're perfect for each other in so many ways. Can't the big lug see that? I can't keep this up, wanting a man who doesn't want to get involved.

So I agreed to go with Con to an independent film because it'll help take my mind off Hudson. I plan on telling Con upfront I just want to be friends.

I even said I'd come to his poetry reading. And yes, you might think I am sending him mixed messages, especially after I told you I didn't want to lead him on. But that's so not the case. I really do enjoy his company. He makes me laugh.

Out of the blue, Hudson calls asking me to come to the winery and help him again. His admin, Jessie, has had an emergency, and Jon's busy doing the lawyerly thing. Of course I said yes. I just have to remember to take it for exactly what it is and nothing more. I'm off to the symphony to hear Dara play tonight. Maybe I will meet someone.

"So what did you think?" Dara asked when she joined Laila in the lobby of Benaroya Hall after the symphony's performance. Dara carried her instrument in a case.

"I'm no expert but I'd say you're a very talented violinist."

Her friend's eyes lit up. "I've been playing violin since I was a child. I've auditioned so many times for a spot on the symphony that I almost gave up. It took me four auditions to finally get a break."

"Perseverance and talent eventually pay off. Have you had dinner yet?" Laila asked.

Dara shook her head. "Didn't have the time to. I was running late. I ate an apple on the way over."

"Then let's get you something to eat," Laila suggested, her hand on her friend's elbow, steering her toward the elevator and underground parking.

Twenty minutes later, and after much circling, they found a restaurant that was still serving dinner at that late hour.

Once they'd placed their orders Laila sat back in the booth and smiled at her friend.

"I really enjoyed getting dressed up and going to the symphony," she said. "I love living where we do, but every now and then it's nice to be in a city and attend a cultural event."

"There's plenty of culture in Seattle and even on the outskirts. There's literally something for everyone here. This city's been called the little New York, and the natives aren't exactly happy about that. That's a pretty bracelet. Where did you get it?"

A slight movement of Laila's wrists set all the charms jangling. For several blissful hours she'd forgotten about Hudson. Now Dara's question brought him back to mind vividly.

"The bracelet was a gift from an old boyfriend," she answered, hoping her tone sounded neutral.

"He sounds special." Dara reached over, capturing Laila's wrist in hers and turning it this way and that. "Nice tattoo. Does the hummingbird have significance?"

"Actually I got it when I was sixteen and quite rebellious. Remember me mentioning both parents were in the navy? My mom gave up her career to be a homemaker."

"Yes, we talked about our similarity in upbringing."

"The tattoo was my way of asserting my independence. I was so sick of moving around. All I wanted to do was put roots down somewhere and be like a normal family. I wanted us to be like the Huxtables. You know, the kids on the old *Cosby Show.* Instead, my dad divorced my mom and took up with the exact type he didn't want her to be—a career woman."

"Isn't that always the way. But you're not exactly traditional Sue, either. You own your own business and you took a risk doing a house swap and coming here. Most women would never leave family and friends and come to a place where they don't know anyone."

"I'm very traditional when it comes to wanting to have a place to call home. Stability and a committed relationship are very important to me. I've been independent most of my life because I never, ever want to have done to me what was done to my mother. I've always wanted to feel connected to someone or something."

"Old-fashioned values in a young body. Today everything's disposable. Things break and we throw them away. Relationships sour and instead of working to fix them we walk away."

Laila sighed. “Don’t I know it.”

The server returned with their meals and the conversation was placed temporarily on hold.

“So tell me about the bracelet,” Dara said, tapping Laila on the wrist and sending the charms jangling again.

It was impossible to get off the topic of Hudson. Bad enough he’d called right before she was heading out the door, practically begging her to help him out.

Dara was now waving a hand in front of her face. “Hey, come back to me.”

“My ex initially bought me the bracelet for my birthday, and a charm for every significant event after.”

“He sounds very kind.”

“He is. At least I thought he was.”

“Said so sadly.” Dara reached for her wrist again. “You still love him, don’t you? It must be hard seeing him when you go off to work at the winery.”

“It is. Can we change the topic? I’m thinking you might like Hudson’s partner, Jon.”

“Tell me about him.” Dara dug into her salad, but her eyes were on Laila.

“They’re both practicing attorneys and they share joint ownership of Jon Hudson Cellars.”

As Laila went on to describe Jonathan Woods, Dara began asking many questions.

“He sounds hot,” she said. “If he’s all that and a

bag of chips, how come you aren't trying to reel him in?"

Almost choking, Laila dabbed at her mouth with a napkin. "Getting involved with a friend of Hudson's would be messy."

"Good point. All right, you're in charge of setting something up."

For the next half hour they exchanged stories about growing up. As they'd earlier discovered they shared a great deal in common, the least of it being families who didn't like putting down roots.

"We should leave." Dara yawned when the server began hovering. "If you'll follow me I'll show you how to get back to Whidbey Island via the bridge. This way you'll know what to do if you ever miss the last ferry."

Laila followed her onto the highway and across Deception Pass Bridge. Although it was pitch-dark now, in the daylight the view must be breathtaking. She'd take this route the next time she went into Seattle and maybe linger a bit admiring the saltwater canyon.

In Langley they went their separate ways. Laila was now more confident navigating the winding roads and hairpin bends. She was home in a matter of minutes. Her dog greeted her with a loud bark before she could step out of the car.

She'd missed his scheduled walk and he had no problem letting her know about it.

"How you doing, boy?" she asked, bending to tickle the mastiff behind his ear. "Want to go for a walk?"

Woof!

Mariner raced off in search of his leash, and Laila quickly stripped off the girly pantsuit and stylish ankle boots she'd worn to the symphony. She replaced the outfit with an old pair of sweats and comfortable sneakers and took the leash from Mariner. Grabbing a flashlight, she put the dog on his leash and headed out.

It would be a quick walk. She'd agreed to show up at the winery tomorrow with the completed copy for Passport to Woodinville in hand. Jessie, Hudson's assistant, was out with another of her family emergencies, for an undetermined length of time, and that's the only reason why Laila had agreed to bail Hudson out. He'd suggested she pack a bag and bring Mariner with her.

Laila had insisted he book a hotel. She couldn't afford a repeat of the other night. She would help with phones and work on the newsletter and Web site updates between calls. By now Hudson should have heard something from the Alcohol and Tobacco Tax and Trade Bureau approving the wine labels. Time was ticking by.

Who would ever have guessed that there were such stringent requirements for designing a wine label? Laila had learned it wasn't just about design.

The brand had to be displayed prominently, and the class, type and designator, meaning red table wine or white, had to be stated on the label. Where it was bottled was also important, as was the alcohol content and the net volume per glass.

She continued her walk in the cold, the fog rolling in as thick as pea soup. Even with a flashlight to illuminate her path, she could barely see in front of her. Eerie night sounds made the whole experience feel like something out of the *Twilight Zone*. Laila allowed Mariner to guide her as her imagination went wild. Was that an owl or was it a coyote on the prowl?

Distracted by the unsettling sounds, and her active imagination on overdrive, Laila tripped over an object and went down hard, losing her hold on the dog's leash. The wind was knocked out of her for several seconds as she lay spread eagle on the ground. Mariner's wet tongue on her cheeks and his concerned whine forced her to her feet again.

She stood, gingerly placing her weight on one foot, and wincing, retraced her steps.

Back at home she applied an ice pack and decided that going to bed might be the best thing for her. Morning would come sooner than she anticipated, and she'd promised Hudson to be at the winery no later than midmorning. She didn't plan on letting him down.

It was too late to call Con and cancel their early-morning walk. She'd leave him a note on the front door and beg his forgiveness.

Next morning the ankle, though still sore, felt much better. Laila made the drive to Woodinville under a leaden sky that looked suspiciously like snow. But snow so seldom happened in Washington State that she was sure it was just her imagination.

"You're limping," Hudson said the moment she came hobbling through the door, Mariner leading the way.

Laila explained about her clumsiness and what had happened last evening.

"Get off your feet right away," Hudson said, quickly pulling out a chair and guiding her into it. "You should have told me you were hurt and I could have hired a temp."

"I'm not exactly incapacitated. There's barely any swelling now. I'll be perfectly fine in a couple of days. My mind and hands work just fine." She booted up the computer, stuck her foot on a carton and sorted through a pile of mail on the desk. Mariner stretched out on the floor, paws under his chin, eyeing Hudson. When her ex-boyfriend straddled the chair across from her, Laila handed him a letter with the words Personal and Confidential written on the front.

"The weather report's not good," Hudson said. "The forecasters are predicting a blizzard. I'm concerned because this area so seldom gets snow that we're not prepared for the removal. Did you pack a bag as I suggested?"

Snow? So she'd been right. It wasn't all in her imagination.

"Yes, my bag is in the trunk of my car. Did you remember to make reservations at a hotel?"

He was either too busy readying the letter or didn't hear her. Surely he couldn't possibly presume that she'd be staying with him again, at least not in his bed.

"Where are you in terms of the copy you're working on?" he asked when he finally tore his eyes away from the paper in his hand.

Laila's attention returned to the monitor. "If you'll give me a minute, I'll print you out what I have, or I can e-mail it if you prefer."

"Print it. It's easier for me to proof that way," Hudson ordered. "We can both look at it together."

The phone rang and Laila reached over to answer.

"Jon Hudson Cellars."

"Is Hudson there?" A woman's irritated voice blasted into her ear.

"May I tell Mr. Godfrey who's calling?"

"It's Talia Chisolm. Who are you?"

"Hudson's assistant," Laila lied, covering the mouthpiece. "Talia Chisolm's looking for you. She sounds awfully cranky."

Hudson groaned. "Talia is the most demanding woman I know. Tell her I'm in a meeting."

"You want me to lie?"

"No, I want you to embellish a little. Aren't you and I in a meeting? We're brainstorming how to move forward with our promotions."

It took a while to get Talia off the line, and even then not until Laila promised to have Hudson return Talia's call the moment he got her message.

"If he doesn't I'll be coming to see him in person," she threatened, before slamming down the phone.

"Whooosh!" Laila exclaimed, repeating the woman's message verbatim.

Hudson responded with a loud groan. Several exaggerated eye rolls followed.

"Have you gotten an update on how the fire was started?" Laila asked, hoping to focus his concentration back on business.

"Nothing that I didn't already know. I did hear from the insurance company earlier. My policy does not cover the cleanup involved, which means more money paid out of our pockets."

"I'm sorry. Look on the bright side of things, at least the building wasn't half-constructed. Can you imagine how much more work would have been involved in getting construction going again?"

Hudson snorted. "It's not something I even want to think about."

"So what are we going to do about Passport to Woodinville?"

He shrugged. "Pray to God that the construction gets up and running soon."

"You might want to think about an alternative plan."

The stress of it all was beginning to tell in his red-streaked eyes and the pinched set to his mouth.

"Can you make a couple of calls and see if there's a company that will clean up the debris? I'm going to call the arson inspector directly and find out if it's safe to move ahead with building." Hudson glanced out the window of his office. "It's coming down already. On the brink of spring this shouldn't be happening."

White cotton balls were falling from the sky like manna from heaven, but at least the snow wasn't sticking yet. It was a good thing she'd packed that bag. Navigating those winding roads later would prove to be treacherous.

"Maybe it's just flurries," she said optimistically. Deep down she wasn't too sure about that. The bare branches of trees were already coated in white. If the temperature fell that snow would turn into ice.

Mariner let out a low belly growl.

"Easy, boy, what's got you so riled up?" Laila asked, scratching the pooch behind the ear.

The front door swung open. A woman covered in fine white particles shook the icicles from her hair and stomped her feet on the mat.

"Am I at the right place?" she inquired.

"That depends," Laila came back with.

Hudson used the interruption as an opportunity to retreat to his office.

Laila smiled pleasantly at the well-dressed woman. "Do you have an appointment?"

"Yes, with Hudson Godfrey, one of the owners of Jon Hudson Cellars. I have an interview scheduled."

"Please have a seat. Your name is?"

"Barbara Manson."

"Let me see if Mr. Godfrey's available."

Laila would bet anything Hudson had forgotten. She took off up the hall and tapped on Hudson's closed door. It took him a moment to open up.

"Barbara Manson's here for an interview. Did you forget about her?" she asked

"Who?"

Hudson's head was down, absorbed in his day planner.

He looked so tired she wanted to reach out and give him a hug. The lines around his eyes had deepened, and she could tell all of these unsettling incidents had taken their toll.

"Barbara says you rescheduled her to today. She's here to talk to you about the tasting-room manager's position."

Hudson gave another glance at his day planner and muttered an oath under his breath.

"I may have screwed up. Jessie would have been

the one to reschedule her, and if she told me about it I forgot. Give me five minutes to regroup and then send her in. Can you get us both some water?"

"I'll give you ten minutes. Meanwhile I'll chat her up and give you my opinion later."

"Great! Personality along with solid credentials is what I'm looking for. A tasting-room manager also has to be a goodwill ambassador."

"I have a pretty good idea what you're looking for. Don't forget Talia Chisolm. She's expecting you to call her back. Snowing or not I wouldn't put it past her to just show up."

Hudson slapped a hand to his head. "The last thing I need today is that woman on my doorstep."

"Do you have a résumé from Barbara Manson?" Laila asked as she was about to leave.

Hudson tapped the desk drawer in front of him. "In here somewhere."

When Laila limped back to the outer room, Barbara Manson was tapping an anxious foot.

"Thanks for your patience. Mr. Godfrey is on a conference call. He'll be with you shortly," Laila said.

Several phone lines were lit up and for the next several minutes she did a juggling act. Although her ankle was beginning to throb again she ignored it.

She'd just shown the candidate into Hudson's office and closed his door when an attractive woman in her late thirties came flouncing through.

She brushed the snow from an ankle-length fur coat and tossed a mane of hair back. Something about her was familiar.

"I'm here to see Hudson," she announced, giving Laila one of those looks that indicated she wasn't worthy of her time.

"And you are?"

"Talia Chisolm. Mrs. Chisolm, actually."

Using the desk to support most of her weight, Laila brought herself up to her full height of five-seven.

"Please have a seat, Mrs. Chisolm," she said to the diva, whose fur coat reminded Laila of a grizzly bear.

Talia ignored her. She headed off in the direction of Hudson's office, saying over her shoulder, "Never mind. I know where to find him."

"You can't just barge in," Laila shouted, hobbling behind her.

"Watch me."

"Not on my watch you don't."

"Try stopping me."

Laila decided rather than wrestling the witch to the floor she'd see how this played out.

Chapter 14

Hudson attempted to wrap up the interview with Barbara Manson with one final question.

"I am being very particular about who I hire. My wine tastings have to be revenue generators as well as memorable events. What can you bring to Jon Hudson Cellars that is different and unique?"

The brunette seated in front of him thought about what he'd said for a moment. "It's not on my résumé but I graduated from clowning school. I entertained at children's parties and found the parents far more demanding than the children. I quickly learned that my job was to entertain both the children and the adults."

"Very insightful of you. You're creative and smart. Is that why I should hire you?"

Barbara reflected for several seconds.

"I can handle just about any crisis that comes up, with or without face paint. I'm a born entertainer and I'm excellent at getting people to open up their wallets. A wine tasting should be both educational and fun but it's also about getting people to buy." She slid a piece of paper across his desk. "Here are some ideas I've jotted down on the subject of making your business prosperous."

The interview had run over its allotted hour and he had a considerable amount to do. Outside the snow was coming down in curtains. Hudson shook the wrinkles from his slacks as he stood.

"You came prepared, Barbara. I like that. Do you mind if I look this over later?"

She shook her head. "Not at all. How long will it be before you make a decision?"

"Probably a day or two. I'll let you know one way or the other."

Hudson shook her hand.

"I really would like this job, Mr. Godfrey," Barbara added. "There aren't too many women in this business and I'm really good."

"I'm sure you are."

The door flew open and a woman in a swaddling fur came flying through. It took Hudson a few seconds to figure out who she was.

"Uh, Talia, I'm in a meeting."

"My business is just as important as hers," she said, positioning herself between him and the candidate.

"Talia, you're interrupting an interview. If you can take a seat outside I'll be with you as soon as I can."

Barbara looked from one to another, quickly backing out of the room, but Talia maintained her ground.

"What's going on with my divorce?" she demanded.

"Have you spoken with Jon?"

"He keeps me informed, but I want an update from you, not some underling."

"Jon's my partner," Hudson informed her again, tight-lipped. He glanced out of the window, noting the snow was coming down heavier than ever. It had settled on the windshields of the cars in the parking lot and sparkled on the ground. The vines they'd planted would never withstand this weather.

"Hudson, are you listening to me?"

"I am. I'm concerned you may not get home because the weather's getting worse by the minute. Jon and I will set up a conference call with you soon. You need to get on the road now while the roads are still drivable."

Hudson took Talia by the elbow, easing her toward the door. At the same time Laila pushed open the door.

"I'm sorry," she said, stepping aside as Talia Chisolm sailed through.

"No need to be, Ms. Chisolm was just leaving."

"I was not..." Talia sputtered.

"The weather channel says we're about to experience an unseasonable blizzard. The reporters are urging businesses to close early so that people can get home before it really starts coming down. Mrs. Chisolm, you may want to get on the road."

Talia Chisolm snorted.

"I'll expect to hear from you later," she said to Hudson, ignoring Laila completely. Gathering her fur around her, she swept out in a huff.

Hudson waited until she was safely out of the parking lot before commenting.

"That woman's not worth the money she's not paying me."

"Then why are you representing her?"

"I committed to it, and for that reason only I'm determined to follow through."

"Scott wants to talk to you once you have a free moment. He's come by several times," Laila commented.

"Is he waiting?"

"No. He said you should call him."

Hudson suspected he knew what Scott wanted to talk to him about. He probably wanted his permission to send the workers home early.

Scott picked up on the second ring. He was usually calm but today he sounded harried.

"It's really coming down out here," he said. "The team's not going to be productive because they're worried about their families. I'm going to send them home."

"Good idea and you should take off, as well. Everyone will get paid for the full day. We'll worry about the vines tomorrow. There's nothing we can do anyway except hope and pray this doesn't set us back too badly."

When Hudson hung up, Laila stood there waiting.

"If you want to leave you can, too," he said.

She nodded. "Is there anything else you need me to do?"

"We'll worry about it tomorrow."

"Okay, I'll need the name of the hotel."

Hotel? What was she talking about? Hudson squeezed Laila's shoulder and immediately knew it was a big mistake. Touching her only made the memories come alive in vivid Technicolor. He'd held her and loved her knowing that there was no immediate future for them, and that just wasn't fair.

"Hudson?"

"I'm sorry, what was it you asked?"

"You did book me a room?"

"I think I might have asked Jessie to."

"And?"

"Pack up and we'll sort out where you're staying later."

As she turned away, Laila's body language said it all. She was really teed off with him. Jessie normally took care of details such as hotel arrangements and transportation, but to be honest he couldn't recall if he'd asked her to make hotel reservations. Laila would be livid when she discovered he'd dropped the ball.

Laila was back, purse in one hand and dog in the other.

"So did you check on my reservations?" she queried. "We'll need a place that takes dogs."

"Uh, not exactly. I'm not sure what Jessie did."

"Then I guess I better get on it."

"Try Woodinville Manor. The business has an account there. The number is on the bulletin board in front of you. Wine Inn is another alternative. I'll gladly call if you'd like."

"Don't bother."

She left to return after several minutes, looking even more irritated.

"There aren't any rooms to be had. Everything's booked because of the weather and they've told me in no uncertain terms they will not take an animal. I guess Mariner and I will be sleeping under this desk."

"Nonsense, there's plenty of space at my house. You'll come home with me."

That produced flames from her nostrils and an audible discharge of breath.

Luckily his cell phone rang and he reached for it.

"Hudson Godfrey here...yes, Jon? How bad are the roads? No, doesn't sound good—Jon's staying in Seattle," he announced, holding the phone away from his ear. "He's not going to even try to make it home. Too dangerous, he says."

After speaking to his partner for a few more seconds he disconnected.

"The weather's that bad?" Laila asked, raising a skeptical eyebrow.

"Yes. Jon says several people have already spun out. He's not going to risk it by coming home. Let's head out. I'll deal with whatever needs to be done tomorrow."

Laila gave him another narrow-eyed glance. He could tell she was still uncomfortable about going home with him. Well now she didn't have much choice.

"Where's that bag you packed?" he asked.

"In the trunk of my car."

"I'll get it while you lock up. The keys are in your top drawer."

Laila turned over her car keys and made sure all the windows in the building were closed and the doors locked. She grabbed Mariner and joined Hudson in the parking lot.

Hudson ran one hand over his head, brushing away the snow that had accumulated. The temperature had dropped by several degrees and the whiteness was now almost blinding. He carried Laila's bag in the other hand.

"Better hang on to me," he said, holding out the crook of his free arm to Laila. "It's going to be one slippery walk home. It looks like it could be a skating rink, and I don't want you reinjuring that ankle."

Given how close the business was to his house, there was no reason to drive to the winery. At times that walk had been a lifesaver and often he'd used it to clear his head. He would sometimes plan his day while getting some much-needed exercise.

But there was no clearing his head today, not with Laila hanging on to his arm and the sides of her breasts brushing against him occasionally, as they both tried to stay on their feet. She was proving to be a major distraction when they started the slippery journey home.

As he went along, Hudson made a mental inventory of the contents of his refrigerator and cupboards. The storm had been unexpected, or he would have stocked up on groceries. At least he could count on canned goods. If nothing else he had soup and tuna fish in abundance.

A walk that normally took ten minutes lasted almost half an hour. Several times they came close to falling but managed to hang on, barely.

Hudson's front porch was a happy sight, even weighted down by snow. Gingerly he started up the incline leading to the front door. In a protective gesture, his grip around Laila's waist tightened. He would never forgive himself if she fell.

Inside the house felt like summer compared to what they'd been through outdoors. Hudson left her and Mariner in the kitchen and went off to start a fire.

"Where should I put my bag?" Laila asked when he returned. She'd taken a seat at the kitchen table.

There was only one place to consider—his bedroom, of course—but telling her that wouldn't serve him well.

"You've got four bedrooms to choose from," Hudson reminded her diplomatically, not exactly putting into words that the fourth bedroom was his. "Pick the one you're most comfortable in. I can at least guarantee fresh linens. My housekeeper is very good at keeping me in check. Have you had lunch yet?"

Laila gave him a look that was hard to read.

"No. There wasn't time. Let's look at the upstairs bedrooms."

"Of course."

He was mindful of her sore ankle. "I'll bring your bag up, and after you pick a room I'll see what I can do about feeding us."

Carrying her bag, Hudson hustled up the stairs

ahead of her while Laila and her dog followed more slowly.

"Bedroom number one," Hudson announced, opening the door at the top of the stairway with a flourish. A window seat looked out through leaded panes onto an awesome winter wonderland in the making. She'd loved this bedroom when he'd given her a tour of the house.

"It's lovely but I'd like to see the others again. The ones you're not sleeping in," she added.

It was his turn to give her a sideways glance.

Midway down the hall he turned the knob on another door of a room he thought was her favorite. "This one has a nice comfortable sitting area with a view of the pond."

"I love it," Laila gushed. "Especially the bed." She pointed to the four-poster draped in tulle.

"It's a girly room but a personal favorite," Hudson said, taking her bag inside and setting it down on an upholstered chair. "I'm going to start lunch and leave you to freshen up a bit."

He was tempting fate having her in his house, because even away from her, Laila's scent still lingered in his nostrils. It would require some discipline to keep his hands to himself. Better get busy putting together that meal.

A quick glance outside confirmed the storm had intensified. Hudson switched on the radio and went about the business of preparing lunch.

He'd just set the salad on the table when a freshly showered Laila emerged dressed in his old bathrobe. Mariner, of course, preceded her. Laila's hair was still damp and hung in a curtain of ringlets around her face. She looked young, beautiful and vulnerable. The sight reminded him of the first time he'd spotted her sitting on that beach.

"I hope you don't mind," she said, pointing to his terry-cloth robe. "I thought a hot shower might warm me up."

"Mind, of course not. I wish I looked as good in that old thing as you do. How's the ankle?" He shoved a chair at her. "Get off your feet. Lunch is coming up in seconds. I hope you like chef salads because that's about all that I have. That and the soup on the stove. Rolls are in the oven. We can eat in a few minutes."

Laila sat on the chair he pulled out for her. She wound a finger around one of the wet strands of her hair, twirling and twirling. It was hard to figure out what she was thinking.

She was driving him crazy. What was under that robe? How could he possibly string two sentences together when he didn't know whether Laila was wearing underwear or not? His mind did register that she smelled heavenly, though. His head was spinning with all of that vanilla.

"I didn't know you could cook," Laila said, smiling at him.

"That's because we were always going out to eat, or you were whipping up one thing or another in that small galley kitchen of yours."

"We did have fun," she said dreamily.

Hudson served their soup in teacups because for the life of him he couldn't find bowls. They were probably still packed in boxes in the garage. He'd been in the house almost two years and there were still items he hadn't unpacked. His total focus had been on the business, and soup bowls were the last thing on his mind.

"This is really good," Laila said, setting down her spoon after she'd finished the last drop.

"You can count on the Pacific Northwest to have good chowder, even if this particular batch comes in a can."

Laila burst out laughing and scooped back a handful of wet hair. She handed him her plate so that he could serve the salad.

"I'm a poor host. I didn't even ask if you wanted something to drink."

"Water would be great and maybe coffee after we're done. I'll even make it."

"No, you won't. You need to stay off that foot."

But she was already on her feet. Hudson was up like a shot, grabbing her by the shoulders and practically forcing her back into her seat. Mariner, not understanding what was going on, emitted a long, low warning growl and bared his teeth.

"It's okay, boy," Laila said, sinking back into her chair and reaching down to smooth the animal's fur. The growling stopped immediately.

"Killer dog you have there," Hudson quipped.

"He looks out for me."

Hudson handed her a bottle of water. The charm bracelet he'd given her jangled as she took it from him. Memories were beginning to surface, and he couldn't allow those memories to cloud his goal. No serious involvements until he was solvent and on his feet.

He sipped on his water, trying to keep his eyes focused on her face and not on the gaping bathrobe that had parted to reveal café-au-lait skin and plenty of cleavage.

Laila was no fool. She sensed where his interest lay.

"What does the weather channel say?" she asked, diverting her attention to the radio he'd turned on low.

Hudson rose to kick the volume up a notch. A fast-talking reporter was giving the latest update:

"If you're traveling North on I5 it's a virtual parking lot. There's a twenty-car pileup and on 405 heading in the opposite direction, a tractor trailer jackknifed. We're talking fatalities here. The roads are an ice rink. I can't stress enough, if you don't need to drive stay put. This storm hasn't even officially begun, folks. For more about road conditions

I'm turning you over to my colleague Jack Madison reporting from Everett..."

"It sounds really bad out there," Laila said, tugging on her lower lip.

"Yes, it does. We won't be going anywhere for a while. After we're through with lunch maybe you'll help me sort through these résumés."

"Sure, but I have my own work, as well. My laptop's in my bag so I won't need your computer."

"How about we work on the newsletter together?" Hudson suggested, daring to meet her eyes. "I'd like to have something in the mail before Passport to Woodinville or at the very least a handout to give anyone participating."

"Okay, that's a plan. The afternoon's still young, there'll be plenty of time. Now let me help you clean up."

"No," Hudson said firmly, shaking his head. "It's gotten very quiet in here all of a sudden."

"Maybe the battery on the radio went dead."

"No, more like a power outage. I better find my flashlights and candles."

As he wandered off, he thought about how fate was playing with him. Work would have at least distracted him. Now he would have to worry about conserving the battery on his laptop and cell phone because there'd be no means to charge it.

And now he'd have to worry about keeping his hands off Laila to boot.

Chapter 15

Laila's Blog
Thursday, March 15

It's going to be one long sexually charged night, I can already tell. Here I am holed up alone in a house with Hudson and we have no electricity. Outside, the snow is coming down like it will never end. There's no television to look at and it will be dark soon, so even reading will be impossible. We could play board games by candlelight, I suppose. That will help pass the time and keep me from thinking of jumping his bones. I gotta go now.

Hudson's heading my way. I'll be sure to tell you how the evening turns out.

"It's really coming down out there," Laila said, snapping closed the notepad she'd been hunched over for the past couple of hours and walking over to the window.

Hudson went to where she was standing and peered out. He groaned loudly and clicked off the remote phone, which thankfully still worked. He remained hanging over Laila's shoulder, peering out into the rapidly growing darkness. She resisted the urge to turn to him and wrap her arms around his waist, seeking the comfort of his broad chest. No, she could not let that happen. Wouldn't.

Laila tried to focus on the trees laden with their bounty of snow. The whiteness had accumulated on the ground in heavy layers at least six inches deep. The sky above was dark and leaden. In a short time outside would be pitch-black. She hoped Hudson found the battery-operated radio soon or the phone would be their only connection to civilization.

The few candles Hudson had found remained on the counter. They'd decided to be conservative and wait to light them.

"I'm going to attempt to make it to the shed and get more wood." Hudson's voice broke through her reverie. "We'll need to keep the fire going all night or it's going to get brutally cold. Without electricity there will be no heat."

"Please be careful. It's really coming down outside. You should take Mariner with you," Laila suggested.

"I just might."

Hudson trotted into the kitchen, and Laila signaled to Mariner to follow. Hudson was already shrugging into his ski jacket and stepping into knee-high rubber boots.

"What about a scarf, gloves, a hat?" Laila asked when Hudson placed his hand on the doorknob.

"Please stop fussing."

"I can't help myself. It's freezing outdoors. You'll come down with pneumonia."

"I'll be fine."

Knowing there was no arguing with him, Laila shrugged her shoulders.

The lure of the outdoors proved too much for her dog. He raced out to frolic in the whiteness, occasionally rolling in it. Laila realized this was his first time seeing snow and he was enjoying it.

Laila pressed her nose to the windowpane, following their progress. She didn't recall a shed out back and hoped that the icy ground didn't prove too treacherous for her two favorite men. For a moment she lost them in the blinding snow but rather than give in to nerves, she boiled water on the gas stove and began making coffee.

Ten minutes went by, and when they still hadn't returned, Laila began to pace. What if something had happened to either one of them? She took in huge gulps of air, willing herself not to panic. If something had happened Mariner would be woofing up a storm.

Finally two dark forms came plodding through the snow. She quickly yanked open the back door, and a paralyzing cold blew in. Laila hugged herself as dog and man trudged up the back steps.

Hudson's teeth chattered as he stomped snow on the mat, while a less restrained Mariner shook his fur, sending icicles and snow everywhere. The canine quickly made a beeline for the fire, wisps of smoke still clinging to his breath.

Laila handed Hudson the coffee she'd poured into a mug.

"Take small sips," she urged, helping him out of the wet coat.

"M-m-man, o-o-h man. It's cold out there," he said when he was able to formulate words, teeth still chattering.

When the phone rang they shot each other curious looks.

"Should I get it?" Laila asked.

"No. I'll get it."

Could be there was a woman on the other end and Hudson didn't want her to find out. It might even be Talia Chisolm. She was certainly pushy enough and Laila would put nothing past her.

Clenching and unclenching his hands to get the circulation going again, Hudson picked up the receiver.

"Hello… Glad you made it. So how did it go? Must have been rough driving, huh?" He listened to the person on the other end for a couple of seconds. "Yes, Laila's here…. No, there weren't any hotel rooms available…. Yes, we can chat about that later."

It had to be Jon on the other end. Laila's mood was buoyed up again. She focused in on the conversation.

"Power's out on Whidbey, too, and the ferries have suspended service. Electricity's out here, as well. It's a good thing you didn't try to make it home…get out…that's not possible. The forecasters are predicting two feet of snow. Yes, remind me to talk to you about Talia Chisolm when this mess is over with."

Hudson hung up and took another sip of his coffee before filling her in.

"Jon got a room at the Mayflower. He says it's really bad in Seattle. The hotel is operating on a generator. Ferry service has been suspended and the side roads are all closed. People are stranded all over and there are many accidents."

"What was that about Whidbey Island?" Laila asked.

"They're not prepared for a storm of this magnitude. The reporters think it might be weeks before the island's back to normalcy, and the worse of the storm hasn't come through yet."

"Aiiiii-ya-yiii."

That could put a big crimp in her plans. She wasn't planning on staying at Hudson's one day longer than she had to. However, as difficult as being in his company was, it would have been worse being alone, especially having to brave a winter storm.

"Light the candles and I'll add more logs to the fire," Hudson suggested. He must have noticed her expression.

"Okay."

Laila found the candles on the kitchen counter. Soon their flickering flames cast an eerie glow around the room.

"We should talk about dinner," Hudson said, coming to stand behind her as she placed two of the lit candles on the mantelpiece.

Turning to respond she bumped into the solid wall that was his chest. The heat kicked up a notch. It had to be the flames from the fireplace. Laila's knees began to slowly knock.

"I'm still full from lunch," she said, hoping the tremor wasn't apparent in her voice. "I'll feed Mariner and then maybe we can talk about your plans for promoting the winery. You'll need some catchy advertising if you're going to compete with the big boys. Let's bounce ideas off each other and narrow down a few to talk to Jon about."

"Okay, but you're officially off the clock," Hudson said, glancing at his watch.

"Ah, so now you're afraid I'll bill you? Don't forget I have a lot invested in your success. It's called royalties."

Hudson's deep laughter rang out, lightening the mood considerably. "How could I forget two to three percent of every sale?"

"Well since I'm here, you might as well pick my brain. I'll trade you marketing experience for room and board."

A loud thud came from outside. Mariner raced toward a window and began a high-pitched keening.

"What the hell?"

Hudson was right behind the dog, and Laila followed on his heels. They peered out the window squinting into the darkness.

"A tree must have gone down," Hudson commented after a while.

"Or an electrical pole. It's hard to tell in the dark."

"No electrical pole, please. That could be a huge nightmare."

The outlook was dismal if that was indeed the case. Being without electricity for days on end was disastrous. Laila knew about what that could easily mean. She'd lived through several hurricanes, having had to move the houseboat to a secure area and move into a hotel. If you weren't a high priority area, the repair could take weeks. She was grateful to Hudson for his hospitality, but she didn't plan on wearing out her welcome.

"I propose we open a bottle of Jon Hudson's finest while we brainstorm our marketing plan," Hudson suggested, heading back to the kitchen.

He returned minutes later with two glasses and a bottle of Merlot in hand and took a seat on the sofa, patting the spot next to him.

"Come on, sit. I don't bite."

With some trepidation Laila joined him on the couch. The rational side of her brain cautioned her to stick to one glass of wine. Two might be pushing it. The spark between them could easily ignite again, blazing more intensely than that coming from the logs spitting in the fireplace.

Alcohol and Hudson were an intoxicating combination. If they were to have any discussion, she needed a clear head. She didn't want Hudson thinking that every time he crooked a finger at her she was his for the taking.

Concentrate, Laila. Focus.

Hudson poured the red wine into two glasses and handed Laila hers.

"To creative thinking," he said, clinking their glasses together.

"I'll drink to that."

Laila sniffed, swirled and savored the liquid the way he'd taught her.

"Exceptional," she pronounced, meaning it.

"Thank you. It's from my special reserve. Jon and I have been working on this concoction for years. We're hoping to introduce it at Passport to Woodinville and hoping that a negociant will put it on their list."

"What's a negociant?"

"He or she is part merchant, part wine maker and part expert taster. They're a professional wine sampler who makes recommendations to wine connoisseurs or just people looking for a different wine-drinking experience."

"Now that's a cool job," Laila said, taking another sip of the full-bodied blend. She set down her glass. "I have an idea."

"I'm open to any thoughts."

She would not read more into his words than what was intended.

"Ever thought of setting up a blending station in the tasting room?"

"And what would I be blending?"

"Custom wines might be the way to go. The more discriminating upmarket patrons would be all over it. They'd love the chance to make their own wines. If you advertised this as a 'Customize Your Own Wine' event, they'd come crawling out of other vineyards. The whole process could take place under the watchful supervision of a wine director and it would be an educational experience for all."

"But this could mean hiring other people and additional overhead..."

Laila held up her hand, stopping him from going on.

"I'm sure there are consultants you could hire for the weekend. Perhaps you could offer a commission on sales."

Hudson's arms wrapped around her. "You may be on to something big, babe. If we gave the folks coming through the tasting room the opportunity to bottle and cork their own creations, they'd then move on to another station to create a custom label. The revenue possibilities could be astronomical. We'd be trendsetters."

Adrenaline surged through her. Laila loved the challenge of coming up with creative ideas.

"It could put Jon Hudson Cellars on the map, especially with an upmarket crowd."

Hudson's finger flicked her cheek. "You keep saying 'upmarket.' Is that the new buzzword for yuppie?" He swallowed on a chuckle.

"Does disposable-income crowd sound better?"

Hudson's laughter rang out as he gave her cheek another finger flick. Laila steeled herself to ignore the tiny flutters beginning at the base of her gut and waking up her hotspots. She took another steadying sip of wine and dared to look at him.

"What else are you thinking?" Hudson asked, edging way too close. His strong thigh muscles now jammed against hers.

"I'm thinking of the best way to advertise this

thing." She closed her eyes. "Maybe something like, Private Moments Deserve a Private Collection." Laila made a wry face.

"Not bad."

"It's mediocre at best."

"What about, Private Moments Deserve a Private Selection?"

"We're getting there."

Hudson's thigh gave hers another brush and the alarm bells clanged. Laila kept her eyes fixed on the fireplace as she raised her glass and took another sip. She was hotter than ever and her entire body twanged.

"This storm's going to affect construction," Hudson groused, taking the conversation off in a completely different direction. "If that tasting room's not ready in time for the festivities, I haven't a clue what I'll do."

"You'll put up a tent and pretend you were holding an outdoor party."

"Now that is an ingenious idea and one I like. It could be a welcome to spring, and we could make the entire experience fun and decorate with tulips."

"You could make it a bacchanal theme. You'd have nymphs pouring wine and wandering musicians serenading the patrons. People are more apt to open their wallets if they feel they're not being sold. And they'll certainly remember Jon Hudson Cellars."

"You are brilliant." Hudson kissed the top of her

head. "This would be different from what everyone else is doing. I have to run the idea by Jon, but I'm confident he'll go for it. You and he think alike, anyway."

Hudson's arms still remained around her. They felt comfortable and familiar. She resisted the urge to lay her head against his shoulders and melt into him. She cautioned herself to remember that she and Hudson were looking for different things. She wanted a man who would put her first above everything, not some guy who'd have her on the back burner until his life was in order.

Hudson's breath was a sweet whisper against her cheeks. Thoughts, ideas, vague concepts coursed through Laila's mind. She'd sort them out later and commit them to paper.

Laila raised her glass and took another sip of wine. The bracelet encircling her wrist jangled.

"I like this wine," she said, getting warmer by the minute.

"Me, too. I wonder what's happening outside?" Taking Laila's hand, Hudson took her to the window.

Outside, a full-blown blizzard was in the making. Snow swirled around like thick curtains, showing no signs of slowing down. Mariner remained in front of the fire, one eye on them.

"Shall we make snow angels?" Laila suggested, half joking. As a child living up north that's what she'd done whenever there was an accumulation.

"Okay, you're on," Hudson surprised her by saying. She'd not thought he had it in him.

"Last one out is a rotten egg," Laila taunted, opening the closet and reaching for her coat.

"You're one crazy woman."

She tossed him his ski jacket then put on her own coat.

"I've never been a wuss."

Mariner scrambled up to join them and bolted out the door. Hudson and Laila carefully eased down the back steps. He had hold of her elbow.

The snow was knee deep already, and to steady themselves they held on to each other. Smoke spiraled upward from their noses and mouths. Pulling away from Hudson, Laila threw herself down into the whiteness and began flapping her arms and legs up and down pretending to fly. Her cheeks burned and her eyes watered but she felt free and without a care in the world. She captured several large snowflakes in her mouth and swallowed them. Even her tongue felt frozen.

"Come on, Hudson!" she called. "Join me."

"Brrrr, brrr, it's cold," he chattered, lying down and making his arms and legs move. A confused Mariner circled them, barking.

"I'm freezing my ass off," he said after a while, struggling into a standing position and reaching out a hand to help Laila up.

Using Hudson as an anchor, together they retraced their steps.

"There's nothing like indulging your inner child," Laila said, hanging on to his arm.

"My inner child is damn cold and a little tipsy."

Back inside again they stood in front of the fire. Hudson insisted they have another glass of wine.

"This should warm us up quickly," he said.

Laila felt carefree and light, even a little giddy. Soon they were giggling uncontrollably and taking a dangerous stroll down memory lane.

"Remember when you took me to Nassau to meet your parents and they wouldn't let us sleep in the same room?" Laila hiccuped.

"How could I possibly forget? Here we were, two grown people sneaking around. We'd wait until they went to bed to creep into each other's room."

"Those were good times, though," Laila said on a sigh. "We were happy. What about the time you and I drove to Naples with no hotel reservations and there wasn't a room to be had. We ended up sleeping on the beach."

"Don't remind me," Hudson said, his arm looped around her neck. "That was the night we almost got arrested. I still have nightmares about that cop tapping me on the shoulder and shining his light in my face."

Hudson's animated recounting of the experience soon had them doubled over in laughter.

"We were so silly. But we had fun." Laila hiccuped again.

"Whose idea was it to make snow angels, mine or yours?"

"Yours. I would never think up anything so juvenile." She threw herself on the rug, imitating what they'd been doing outdoors. "You mean like this?"

Joining in the fun Hudson flopped down beside her, wrapping his arms around her. Soon they were rolling around. When he sneaked a kiss it was all over with. Passion ignited and clothing started coming off in little bits.

Mariner, who watched from his post in front of the fire, didn't seem overly concerned. What Hudson did with his hands stoked an even bigger fire than the one warming the house. His hands were all over her; his fingers probing her sweet spot. If they continued like this there would be no turning back.

All of Laila's concerns were pushed to the back of her mind to take out and examine later. Using her hand she pleasured him. Their lovemaking continued fast, furious and urgent. She refused to think, because thinking would mean the regrets would start rolling in.

Regrets she would deal with tomorrow.

Chapter 16

A week later Hudson stirred in bed. He flung out an arm reaching for Laila. Both eyes popped open when his hand connected with an empty spot. As consciousness invaded, he refused to acknowledge that a piece of him felt as if it was missing. There was no dog whining to go out, and no warm body next to his. It sank in. Laila had take Mariner and gone home to Whidbey Island.

She'd rushed out the door the moment her friend Dara called telling her that parts of Whidbey had both electricity and phone service. She'd said she needed clean clothes and a number of personal things. He couldn't blame her, he supposed. It had been a whole week without electricity. That thud outside had been an electrical pole falling, and the repair crew still hadn't come out.

Thrown together for that short space of time, he and Laila had reconnected and bonded. That probably wasn't such a good thing, given that he still wasn't in a position to do anything about them. Maybe if Passport to Woodinville went as he hoped.

He forced himself to get out of bed, pay bills and do some projects around the house, returning long-overdue phone calls and cleaning out the room he used as a home office. Anything not to think of Laila.

Despite seeing each other at their absolute worst, they'd had a few laughs. Hudson had groused about shoveling snow but Laila had simply grabbed a shovel and done her part. He'd complained about not having a variety of foods to eat and that he was sick of eating from cans. She'd gone through the refrigerator, collected the leftovers and whipped up a concoction on a barbecue grill. They'd found humor in the situation and made time to frolic. They'd made love several times and that had brought them even closer, or so he'd hoped.

The winery was still officially closed. Most of the workers lived in remote areas that remained unplowed, making it treacherous to drive. After conferring with Jon they'd decided to pay their employees anyway. No way could they penalize them for an act of God.

Progress, of course, had come to a halt on the tasting room. Hudson had written off salvaging any of the vines, and that was going to hurt. He was accruing expenses with very little coming in. Since all the major companies and municipal buildings were still closed, there wasn't much going on with his legal business. Clients' issues were placed on hold, and that translated into fewer billable hours. If something didn't turn around for him soon they would have serious financial problems.

Refusing to indulge in a pity party, he peered out of the window. Outside was gray and bitter-looking. The leftover snow had a yellowish tinge to it now as if some gigantic beast had used it as a urinal.

Hudson's landline rang as he indulged in another cup of coffee.

"Yes?" he growled, not even attempting to be civil.

"Good morning. It's Scott, sorry to be calling this early."

"How you doing, man?"

His vineyard manager hadn't been in since the snowstorm. He'd been snowed in and without electricity.

"Holding up. I'm going to try to come in today. The major streets in my area are finally plowed. It's the side streets that are still a mess."

"What about electricity?"

"We're still out."

"There's not much going on here so why don't you take today off, as well. The roads are still icy and I doubt you're going to be able to salvage any vines at this point. We can't do much without electricity. I'm answering phones and keeping an eye on the place."

"Only if you're sure. I thought it might be a good morale booster for my people to see me come in."

"Not too many of your people are here," Hudson informed him. "Jon finally made it in from Seattle a couple of days ago, and he said he barely missed spinning out on the icy side roads. I'd rather you wait."

"In that case I really can use the extra day or so to clean up the yard. I'll see you first thing tomorrow."

Forty minutes later Hudson was seated behind his desk at Jon Hudson Cellars. An hour later Jon showed up wearing a turtleneck sweater and jeans that had seen better days. He stepped out of rubber boots and laced on his sneakers.

"Where's Jessie?" he asked, looking around.

"I haven't heard a word from my admin in several days, and I've been too busy to check on her. She might have tried reaching me on my cell, but without electricity her messages are going nowhere."

"The landlines still work. I would have thought she'd be more responsible. I gave my cell a good long charge before I left the hotel. Since then it's been the car's cigarette lighter for me."

"That's not a bad idea. I'm surprised we haven't heard from Talia Chisolm by now. I'm sure she's already left several messages. Has she tried reaching you? She showed up here raising hell."

Jon groaned. "That woman can drive any man to drink. It might well explain her problems with her ex."

"Tell me about it."

"Any more men show up for work?" Jon asked, heading into his office.

"We're operating on a skeleton crew. Without electricity there's very little we can do."

"It'll all work out," Jon, the eternal optimist, called from inside the room.

"Shouldn't we talk about whether or not we still want to open to the public at the end of April?" Hudson asked, following him.

Jon's eyebrows flew ceiling-high. "You're not thinking of backing out of Passport to Woodinville?"

"I'm not sure we'll be ready."

"Come on, bro. It's our one shot to recoup some of the money we've already sunk into this place. Give me an hour to get caught up and then we'll sit down and come up with a plan."

After an hour had gone by, Jon appeared in Hudson's office. He straddled a chair and faced his partner.

"What's the final word on the insurance claim?"

"The policy only covers buildings and contents. We're stuck paying for the cleanup."

Jon swore under his breath. "Another expense we don't need."

"Tell me about it. Its been labor problems, a man hurt on the job, a fire, the health inspector up our butts and now a winter storm that's shut everything down. When does it end?"

"It ends with us being our own bosses and having a legacy to pass on to our families. Something good has to come out of adversity."

"Let's hope so. Did I tell you about Laila's idea for a bacchanal?"

"No. Run it by me."

Hudson described the festivity that Laila had proposed. He went on to tell Jon about her other idea for the blending station.

"Now, that's awesome and a potential money maker to boot."

"I agree," Hudson said. "Given everything that's gone down so far, I'm stumped as to how we should move forward."

"First we need to figure out where this blending's supposed to take place. I doubt we'll have a tasting room in place."

"Laila suggested renting a tent."

"That's another great idea. That woman is full of them. Maybe you should consider keeping her around." Jon gave Hudson a sideways glance.

Truthfully Hudson would have liked nothing better, but right now he needed all of his emotional energy to go into making the winery a success.

"We have approximately one month to get our acts together," Jon said, breaking into his thoughts.

"Not a lot of time."

"Enough if we're strategic and organized."

Jon outlined a plan to get them there.

Hudson pursed his lips, thinking on it. "That's feasible and could work. Let's just hope the money we sink into getting the place cleaned up and operational isn't wasted money."

Jon slapped Hudson's back. "Think positive. We're already in too deep. What's happening with the copy Laila was to have ready? Is she planning to come back in this week?"

Hudson shrugged his shoulders, "I don't know. She did some work longhand, but without electricity and a computer she may have gotten behind. She did say she would e-mail me the finished product the moment my electricity came on."

"We should check up on her and see how she's doing. The mailing needs to be out at the latest next week, especially if we want people to put us on their calendars. I'm thinking we should make the trip to Whidbey tomorrow. What do you say?"

What could he say? Deep down he wanted to see Laila, even be with her. But pride got in the way.

Not until he had something substantial to offer her was he willing to give her hope.

Someone had shoveled Laila's driveway and that made it easy to enter the cottage. She owed whoever it was big-time. Driving back had had its challenges and now she was really looking forward to clean clothing, putting her feet up and enjoying a nice cup of Seattle's finest.

The inside of the cottage was ice-cold. Hopefully the pipes had not burst. After setting down her bag, Laila checked to see if the lights came on. She held her breath as she flipped the switch. When the lamps illuminated she did a little jig. Electricity meant hot food and a warm shower, luxuries she hadn't enjoyed in days.

She cranked up the heat, left Mariner in his favorite spot and began disrobing. Her ankle was completely healed by now and she practically raced down the short hallway to the shower. Twenty minutes later she emerged feeling better than she had in a long time. It felt good to be able to shampoo her hair.

It would be useless checking phone messages. With the electricity out, the answering machine wouldn't have picked up.

Laila was sipping on coffee and waiting for a pot of water to boil when the doorbell rang. She'd been considering making herself a nice bowl of pasta and taking it with her to one of the wing chairs, propping her feet on an ottoman and watching television, though she'd never been much of a television watcher before. Even so, once that option had been taken away from her, she missed it.

She stared at the pot, willing the water to boil, and decided to add a dribble of olive oil. When the doorbell rang she automatically assumed that it was Dara.

"Hey, girl," she greeted as she threw open the door. "Uh, Con, what are you doing here?"

Con Austin was huddled into a down jacket with a hood that tied under the chin. His hands were stuffed into his pockets.

"I stopped by to make sure you were okay," he said. "You were gone awhile. I was worried."

Laila's eyebrows knitted together in puzzlement. "Didn't I leave you a note?"

"You did, stating that you wouldn't be available for our walk but you didn't say how long you would be gone."

"I'm sorry."

Con was still standing on her threshold. Good manners dictated she let him in. She moved aside.

"Come in out of the cold."

Truthfully she was not in the mood for company. She'd been so looking forward to a relaxing evening, giving her time to mull over the events of the last several days.

Con entered the vestibule, looking around.

"It's still chilly in here, do you need me to help you light a fire?" he asked.

"I just cranked up the heat. It should warm up in a few minutes."

He shrugged out of his coat, and she took it from him and hung it in the closet.

"If I got a fire going it might help," he said.

Laila hoped he was not planning a long visit.

"Okay. The starter logs are over there." She pointed to a spot on the other side of the mantelpiece. "There's wood on the back porch under the tarpaulin."

Con went off to get the wood and Laila added pasta to the water. Maybe if he saw she was in the middle of preparing her dinner that would be that.

Con returned, logs in hand, and set about lighting the fire. Laila felt obligated to at least offer him a drink.

"How about coffee, Con, or maybe you'd prefer something stronger?"

"Coffee's good."

Yes, he did plan on hanging out.

While Laila brewed coffee, Con settled into a wing chair in front of the fire.

"I was really concerned," he said after a while. "You've been gone over a week. I kept checking on your place, and when there were no signs of life I had your walkway shoveled."

"That was you? That was really very nice. Thank you."

"I was just being neighborly. You're a single woman. I figured it's scary enough not having electricity and no real means of communicating with the outside world, on top of that no access to your home."

Laila felt she owed him some sort of explanation. Con had been concerned and he'd gone out of his way for her.

"Remember me telling you I had a client who owned a winery?"

He steepled his fingers under his chin and nodded.

"Yes, I recall you mentioning it."

"Well I went in to do some work for him and got stuck in Woodinville."

"That might have been a good thing. It wasn't fun and games here. There are some areas still in darkness. If you didn't have a generator you were out of luck."

Laila handed Con his coffee. She'd almost forgotten about the pasta on the stove and raced to turn the burner off.

"Am I disturbing your dinner?" Con said with amazing sensitivity.

"No, not really. I can put up more pasta if you like."

She felt obligated. After all, he'd really been quite nice, shoveling the snow from her front door.

"How about I take you to dinner?" Con countered.

Going out was the last thing she felt like but how to politely decline?

"May I have a rain check? I really hadn't planned on being gone for such a long time. I'm edgy and tired, and I'd planned on vegging tonight and watching whatever captures my fancy on television. Join me if you'd like."

Con set his coffee cup down and stood.

"I think I have taken up enough of your time. I'll give you a couple of days to get settled, and then maybe we can resume our walks again."

"Call me," Laila said, handing him his coat.

The telephone rang as she walked with him to the door. She decided to let the answering machine pick up.

Hudson's voice on the tape made it impossible. The pulsing began again in all of her erogenous zones. Laila raced off to answer the phone.

Too late—he'd already hung up.

She replayed his message:

"Hey, I just wanted to make sure you made it home safely. I'm hoping to have electricity back in a day or two. Let me know if you need anything. Jon and I are here for you."

Disappointment sank in. There was nothing warm or fuzzy about what he had to say. He was doing what any decent guy would do. She'd been hopeful he would come to his senses and realize that what they'd had was special, but from his words he could have been checking on the next-door neighbor.

The pasta was mushy by now. Hoping to steady her nerves, she opened a bottle of sauce and poured red wine into a glass tumbler. The bracelet at her wrist jangled, setting off a chain of difficult memories. It was definitely time to move on. In a defiant motion Laila tugged at the clasp and the bracelet fell. She left it where it was, tossed the pasta into the sink and took her red wine with her.

Maybe she should have accepted Con's invitation. What could it have hurt? He at least seemed interested in her, at least interested enough to be fairly persistent. It wasn't as if he was calling her up expecting her to do things for him.

Laila was pouring another glass of wine when the doorbell chimed again. So much for an evening of sitting back and chilling.

She opened the door to find Dara on the other end, and she hugged her friend.

"I'm so glad to see you."

"And I you."

Perhaps what she really needed was another woman's perspective on things.

Dara would tell her the truth.

Chapter 17

Laila's Blog
Thursday, March 29

I really like Dara. She's got a good head on her shoulders. She also helped me put perspective on the Hudson situation. She thinks it's that caveman thing going on. Men are hunters, protectors, that sort of thing. She says it's Hudson's ego getting in the way and that he doesn't want to be involved at this point because he feels he has nothing to offer me.

I felt good after talking to her, but I'm still not of

a mind to hang around waiting for a man to wake up and realize it's not material things I'm after. I want his heart, body and soul. Hudson's not an indigent living under a bridge. He's an attorney, educated and with the ability to earn a living. Even if the winery goes bankrupt, he has something to fall back on.

On an entirely different note, Dara wants me to introduce her to Jon. They'd be perfect together. She'd loosen him up a bit. We'll see if I can pull that off.

I gotta go. Someone's knocking on my door.

"Laila, are you there?"

The insistent banging on the front door finally got Laila's attention. Mariner was off and running, his ears twitching and his nonexistent tail attempting to wag.

"Easy, boy, I'm right behind you," Laila called after him.

Reluctantly she took her hands off the keyboard. The muffled voice outside was male and sounded familiar. She'd been glued to her laptop these last couple of days trying to catch up on work for other clients and trying to meet Jon Hudson's tight mailing deadline.

She'd e-mailed the final draft of their copy for approval, but the last time she'd checked there'd been no response, probably because there still wasn't power.

"Laila, if you're home open up."

Laila's heartbeat escalated. There must be something wrong with her hearing. No way was it Hudson. Her bets were on Con since she'd blown him off and not met him for their agreed-upon walk. She'd been too busy.

"Who is it?" she asked before sliding the bolts.

"It's Hudson and Jon."

Oh, God, no. She'd been right after all. What were they doing here?

"Give me a minute."

The tightening in her chest increased and the pounding moved to her ears. Laila's knees were literally knocking. Jon and Hudson were the last two people she expected to see. She was a mess. Earlier that morning she'd thrown on an old pair of sweats and thick athletic socks to keep her feet warm. She'd braided her hair and ignoring the mess around her, glued her butt to a chair. She'd been banging words out all day. There was no time to pick up now, not with the two men already on her front steps.

Laila wiped her hands on the knees of her sweats and tugged the bill of the baseball cap low. Mariner's tongue lolled out as he made anxious circles around her. A low keening came from deep within his belly.

"This is a nice surprise," Laila said when she tugged the door open. "What brings you to me?"

Hudson rubbed gloved hands together. Cold air curled from his nose and mouth. It was Jon who answered.

"We thought we would check on you to make sure you were okay and had everything you needed."

It was Jon's idea, not Hudson's.

"We tried to call but all we got was voice mail," Hudson added.

There was a slight pinkish tinge to Hudson's bronze cheeks. He tugged off his wool cap and smoothed a leather-gloved hand over his short hair. Jon stomped his feet on the front mat, reminding Laila of her manners.

"Please come in!"

She stood aside remembering that in order to concentrate she'd left her cell phone turned off. She'd been checking her messages every few hours.

Both men stood awkwardly in the vestibule. Mariner circled them, occasionally licking their hands.

"Let me have your coats." Laila held out her hands, waiting.

She took the wool coats the men thrust at her and hung them in the closet.

"This is a cool setup," Hudson said, eyeing the vibrant Peter Maxx paintings on the walls and the earth-tone hemp rugs on the wooden floors.

"Why don't I show you around?"

They would just have to deal with the dirty dishes, the magazines in piles and her unmade bed. She wasn't going to even apologize.

As Laila whisked them through the house, the men stopped occasionally to admire an antique piece. Brock Lawrence, the man she'd swapped with, had exquisite taste and an eclectic way of decorating.

"Looks like you've settled in," Hudson commented as they returned to the living room where they'd started.

"More or less."

No need to elaborate further. Laila tugged on the bill of her cap and found she missed her jingling bracelet. Taking it off symbolized she'd move on.

Hudson's eyes were fastened on her wrist.

"Aren't you missing something?"

"What?"

"Your bracelet?"

So he'd noticed.

"The clasp broke," Laila fibbed.

No need for him to know that in a fit of despair, or was it frustration, she'd ripped it off and relegated it to the bottom of her jewelry box. It was no longer a symbol of Hudson's love but a painful reminder of what they once had been to each other. She was sick to death of holding on and hoping he'd come to his senses.

She gestured to two chairs in front of the fireplace and pulled up a seat for herself. Once the men were seated, Mariner draped himself across Hudson's ankle.

"Did you get your electricity back?" Laila asked when a prolonged silence ensued.

"Yes, early this morning, finally."

"Being out of power has got to have hurt business."

Hudson nodded and tugged on his lower lip. "I'm trying not to think about it."

Better to leave well enough alone, she decided.

"So you probably haven't had a chance to look at what I sent you," she said, her eyes trained on Jon since looking at Hudson was proving to be too painful an experience.

"Actually we have," Jon said smoothly, removing copies from an envelope he was carrying. "We talked about it as we drove. You did a superb job, if I may say so. It's ready to go."

Laila made a production of batting her eyelashes at them.

"So glad my copy passed inspection. Did you want me to handle the mailing? I can bill you later, after you get some money in."

"If you'd handle the mailing that would be great. We'll send you our mailing list," Jon said.

Hudson was looking directly at her. She could feel that electric pull again. She lowered her eyes to avoid making the connection.

"How long did it take you to shovel out?" he asked.

"I was lucky. When I got home the walkway was clean."

She could hear his brain going click, click, click, calculating what she'd just said.

"Then you must have made friends."

"A few here and there. Coffee?" Laila asked brightly, pushing the memories of his hands on her body aside.

Both men nodded but it was Jon who spoke up. "That would be great."

When Laila went off to make coffee, her front doorbell rang. She was being overrun with visitors today.

"I'll get it," Jon offered, heading for the door, leaving her alone with Hudson who followed her into the kitchen.

"I've missed having you around," he said, leaning a hip on the kitchen counter.

"I thought you'd be happy to have your space back. Isn't it fish and guests that stink after three days?"

Hudson's long low chuckle made the tremors start again. His fingers clasped her wrist, tugging her closer. "So what's the real deal with the bracelet?"

He had no right to bring that up and the memories of the good times they'd had. He was really starting to frustrate the hell out of her.

Jon's appearance saved her from responding.

"You have a visitor," he announced, a wide grin

on his face, his almost jet-black eyes lighting up. "She's a rather attractive woman, says her name is Dara. Is she single by chance?"

Laila placed a hand on her hip and angled an eyebrow at him. "Yes, she's single. Why?"

"Let me rephrase the question. Is she available?"

"As in, is she dating someone? Why don't we ask her?"

She tromped out to the living room, the men behind her. Dara was already comfortably seated on the couch. Her Chihuahua, Fiesta, resided on Mariner's paws.

"I was worried about you," Dara greeted, springing up and flinging her arms around Laila. "When you didn't answer your cell I thought I'd come by. I hope you don't mind."

Laila returned her new best friend's tight hug.

"Of course I don't mind. I should have checked in with you but I've been so busy catching up. Meet Jon. This is Hudson Godfrey, his partner."

Dara's clear gray eyes met Hudson's head-on. "Nice to meet you, Hudson. Hi, Jon. I'm just grateful not to have to go into Benaroya Hall today."

"Benaroya Hall?" Jon echoed, sounding awed. "Were you going to hear a concert?"

"No. I'm a violinist with the symphony."

"You don't say. I'm impressed. Perhaps you'd consider playing at the winery's upcoming bacchanal."

Dara looked as if he'd just handed her keys to the winery. Her gray eyes were on Jon's athletic physique.

"I'll gladly help in any way I can."

"Jon's also an attorney," Laila volunteered.

"You are?"

Dara gave him another wide-eyed girly look.

"I have an idea," Hudson surprised Laila by saying. "Why don't we go out to a late lunch courtesy of Jon Hudson Cellars?"

"What do you say, Dara?" Jon chimed in, his attention on the attractive violinist.

Behind their backs Hudson and Laila exchanged looks. Without verbally communicating, they were thinking the same thing. Jon and Dara were definitely feeling each other.

Dara was already tugging on her hat and slipping into the coat Jon held out.

"There must be some great places to have lunch," Jon commented, taking his and Hudson's knee-length coats from the closet.

"The Sound Out is a personal favorite and not too long a drive from here," Dara said, her eyes still on Jon's.

Jon was looking at Dara as if she were the sky, moon and stars.

"If you'll give me five minutes to get myself together I'll be right back," Laila said, exiting.

She did a quick change and grabbed her coat

from the closet. When Hudson smoothed out her collar, the tips of his fingers brushed against the sides of her throat. Laila tried not to shudder. This was about a physical attraction and nothing more.

Dara sat up front next to Jon as he drove. Hudson and Laila were relegated to the back of the SUV, their shoulders brushing against each other. Laila had never been so glad to escape any vehicle.

The pastel building perched on the edge of a cliff had an upstairs deck still full of snow, and frost sparkling off the floor-to-ceiling windows. Icicles hung from the railings and balustrades.

Inside was packed, probably because most people had just gotten their electricity back, or were sick to death of being confined indoors.

"There's a twenty-minute wait," the young hostess with pink hair said when they approached.

"Do we want to wait?" Hudson asked the group in general.

"It's probably going to be the same deal anywhere we go," Dara answered. "I vote we wait the twenty minutes. We can go to the bar and get acquainted."

Hudson took the buzzer from the hostess and followed Dara into the crowded bar. The noise level was high and the energy vibrant. It took a while to get the bartender's attention.

Taking their drinks with them, Dara and Jon edged into a corner. They seemed to forget anyone else existed. Without them as buffers, an uncomfortable silence descended.

Laila felt as if she was on a first date, with the stress level high and wondering whether the evening would end with a kiss or if the man would ask her out again. There was fat chance of any of that happening.

"This was a great choice," she said, breaking the silence. She looked around at the cherrywood panels and the roaring fire in the fireplace. There was a wonderful hickory smell. Framed newspaper articles adorned the walls.

"Yes, it's got personality and warmth."

"Much like Dara, wouldn't you say?"

They both smiled, getting it. There was still so much that remained unsaid between them. Once upon a time conversation flowed easily and without censoring.

"Was it rough getting here?" Laila asked, resorting to small talk.

Hudson sipped on his drink and contemplated. "So-so. Most of the main roads are clear, but traffic was a nightmare with people trying to get abandoned cars home. Jon was really worried about you."

Jon, not him.

"Jon and I have always gotten along. He's a very caring man."

Hudson attempted to pull his foot out of his mouth.

"Jon isn't the only reason I came, Laila. I wanted to make sure your home was okay and that you didn't need my assistance."

"That was thoughtful of you."

They were dancing around, reduced to banalities, this man she'd slept with and been intimate with.

"Have you gotten much copywriting done?" he asked.

Bingo! The real reason Hudson had come. This was about business and not at all about her.

"Actually, yes. It helps to have electricity and virtually no distractions."

"I know what you mean."

The buzzer in Hudson's hand vibrated.

He waved the lit wand at Dara and Jon before offering Laila his arm.

Tamping down on the bittersweet feeling that his touch evoked, Laila hooked her hand through the crook. She must remember to keep their relationship strictly business. By continuing to sleep with him she was sending him mixed messages, too.

And that needed to stop.

Chapter 18

Three weeks went by quickly and for once everything seemed to be going well. The snowstorm had caused some damage and inconvenience but all in all it could have been worse. Even some of the vines had survived. For the past week or so the workers had been blending, bottling and labeling in preparation for the Woodinville Weekend. It would be better to have too many bottles on hand than not enough.

Construction had resumed, but the tasting room was still nowhere near completion. Those weeks of bad weather had really set them back. The plan was to rent a party tent just as Laila suggested and turn it into a tasting and blending area.

On the Saturday of the festivities, Hudson rose early and took a leisurely walk over to the winery as was his custom. He wanted to get there before the first employee showed up. He figured it would give him time to walk the property and figure out a contingency plan for any unexpected situations.

This weekend was a make-or-break one. Word of mouth could drive business. He'd spent far more than he'd budgeted on flowers, professional musicians, entertainers and extra staff. He'd wanted the bacchanal to rival any that the Greek gods might have had. He'd even hired vans for those who had imbibed too much and didn't have designated drivers.

Breathing in the crisp morning air, Hudson walked his property. He had a good four hours before the place would be overrun by people, or so he hoped. Employees would arrive in the next two hours and that included the hired staff. Hopefully, sales would be good and they'd take in more than they'd put out.

He'd advertised the heck out of the event. His employees were pumped and excited, and he and Jon were pumped. Now all he needed was people talking up Jon Hudson Cellars and putting their money where their mouths were.

He arrived at the place where the tent was supposed to be. There was no tent. What had gone wrong? He'd left the men putting up the tent when he left last evening. If there had been a problem you would think they'd let him know.

Horrified, Hudson looked down, spotting the canvas folded like an accordion on the ground. His immediate assumption was that the rental company had done a lousy job of erecting the tent. He'd call them and give them a piece of his mind and get them back out here to take care of business. The effect would have been disastrous if they'd already had stations set up.

He became even more irritated when he grabbed a fistful of the collapsed canvas only to discover the material had huge holes in it. The enormity of the situation quickly dawned on him.

"Son of a—!" Although he seldom cursed, a string of crude expletives followed. Something like this warranted it.

Things had been going too perfect up until now. He examined the material more closely. It looked like someone had taken a knife to the leased tent, deliberately destroying it. He needed to make a quick decision because in the blink of an eye wine lovers would be all over his premises.

He'd advertised a tasting room with a blending station. He'd hired musicians and constructed a temporary dance floor. Servers would be wandering around in togas; mimes would be entertaining the young adults. And there would be no tasting room.

Hudson's hands clasped the top of his head as he examined his options. It was too late to cancel the festivities, and even if that option were available, he couldn't afford it. The smart thing to do was absorb the cost of the destruction and try to rent another tent.

At this point it was crystal clear his string of bad luck was no accident. Someone must have it in for him and Jon. And now they were getting bolder. Hudson took a quick look at his watch. Maybe the party store where they'd rented the destroyed tent would already be open. They'd have to pay for the first one, of course, and persuade the store to rent them another. If the service provider was able to get someone over on the double, they might still be able to salvage the day.

Hudson snatched his cell phone from his waistband and stabbed a button.

"Hey, Jon, are you on your way over?"

"I'll be there as soon as I finish my coffee."

"Bring your coffee with you."

"Something up, bro?"

"I'll tell you when you get here."

"I'm on my way."

When Jon hung up, Hudson stabbed another set of numbers, this time calling the police. From what he could tell, this was vandalism and needed to be reported. His jaw clenched as he felt himself getting madder.

Where was Scott Wilkinson when he needed him? He'd promised to come in early, and so did the newly hired tasting-room manager, Barbara Manson. Hopefully the police would respond in a speedy manner. There was only a small window of time before the winery's gates were officially open.

Hudson raced back to his office, found a disposable camera in the desk drawer and returned to the site to take photos. By then two police cars had pulled up, and the cops were circling the scene and mumbling in low voices.

Spotting Hudson, a heavyset cop approached.

"Mr. Godfrey, when did you discover the tent had been vandalized?"

"Just a little before I called you."

"You've had some trouble before, haven't you?" he asked, scribbling in a book. "Wasn't there a fire on the property recently?"

"Yes, there was."

"Are you the sole owner of the business?"

"Actually, no. I have a partner."

"Where is your partner?"

Hudson felt as if he were being hammered.

"He's on his way."

Where were they going with the questions? It was probably better to keep his answers short and to the point.

"Do you have any enemies that you know of, Mr. Godfrey?" The same burly cop asked.

"None that I'm aware of, although if you're running a business you inevitably make a few."

"What about disgruntled employees?" the African-American officer asked.

"Every company has unhappy employees."

"Would you say they were unhappy enough to light a fire and slash a tent?" This came from the burly one again.

Enough, already. If he had a clue who it was, he wouldn't have called them in. He'd be handling this himself.

Hudson kept his voice even. "That I couldn't tell you."

A thought gnawed at the back of his mind. All the trouble had started when Linton Estates, the winery up the street, began pilfering his people. But Norm Linton, the owner, was a nice, affable guy. He'd been very open about sharing his experiences and challenges.

Besides, Jon Hudson Cellars wasn't exactly competition for Linton Estates, at least not yet. Norm's winery was twice the size of Hudson's, and Hudson hadn't held it against Norm for stealing his people. The majority had come running back looking for their jobs as soon as they realized what having no benefits meant. None had been taken back.

The cops were now circling the site, taking notes and speculating. The plainclothes detectives were snapping pictures and searching the surrounding area for clues.

Jon's arrival caused them to pause.

"Holy sh— What happened here?" The normally cool and collected Jon was visibly upset.

Hudson met him halfway.

"This is what I found when I arrived."

Hudson made the introductions.

"We'd like to ask you some questions," Burly said.

Was that a sympathetic look the African-American officer threw them?

After running his palms over his head, Jon pulled himself together.

"Whatever you'd like."

While he was being interrogated, Scott Wilkinson arrived. He came leaping out of his car and bounding over.

"Tell me this isn't what I think it is."

"Whatever you're thinking is exactly what it is," Hudson answered.

"Oh, man." Scott glanced anxiously at his watch. Hudson could almost hear his mind racing. "We need a backup plan."

"The festivities are due to start at eleven but people have a habit of arriving way before then. We'll need to get this stuff cleaned up almost immediately and we'll need a contingency plan," Hudson said.

Efficient as always, Scott was ready to step

into his role. He'd turned out to be an asset and very dependable.

Hudson continued, "My thought was to rent another tent or maybe several huge umbrellas. We could put signs up designating areas for tasting and blending. Thankfully the Weather Channel is predicting nice weather or we'd be up the creek."

"I'll take off and start scouting around," Scott offered. "I'll use the corporate credit card if I find anything that will work."

"Okay, that's your assignment for the next hour or so. Meanwhile, I'll get this place cleaned up."

"Barb's here," Scott shouted over his shoulder as he loped off. "Have her head up the cleaning effort."

As the minutes ticked by and more and more employees showed up, the cops began questioning them. In the middle of this chaos Laila and Dara arrived.

Hudson had never been so happy to see anyone in his life. He'd felt as if he was drowning in a vat of his own grape juice. He could count on Laila to help find a creative solution to a hopeless one.

She must have realized something was wrong because she came charging across the grounds. Her friend Dara, the violinist, following more slowly behind her.

"What's going on?" she asked, her golden eyes widening in concern.

Hudson pointed to the rags on the ground that were what remained of the tent.

Laila said nothing for a while and then she sprung into action, wrapping her arms around him in a tight hug. She'd always been the demonstrative type and not afraid to show her feelings.

"Oh, Hudson," she said. "This is awful. I thought you'd beefed up security."

"I hired additional help through midnight. Someone must be watching this place closely."

Laila glanced down at the tattered pieces of canvass on the ground and then back at him. "I'm just so angry I could spit! We'd better get moving." She pranced over to the officers. "Are you almost finished? We have a show to put on. Can we clean up?"

Laila's energy got everyone else moving and motivated. An awed Dara stood off to the side watching her friend operating like a whirling dervish.

Once they'd gotten the nod that it was okay to clean the area up, the police left. Barbara Manson's team then sprang into action while Jon and Hudson hotfooted it back to their office.

In less than an hour the toga-clad entertainment would be here, and there was still so much that needed to be accomplished. They were having guided tours of the winery, and the food stations still needed to be set up.

Caterers would be arriving with a smorgasbord any moment. The plan was to have wandering musicians and Greek gods and goddesses pouring wine.

The weekend was advertised as a fund-raiser but all the vintners were hoping that they would make a profit from sales. Hudson was hoping that the bacchanal would be so well received that by the time the official release date rolled around they'd be a household name.

Scott returned looking rather pleased with himself. He'd been able to find two smaller tents, both big enough to provide shelter and a place to custom blend and taste. For the next few hours they worked like dogs and by the time the first person drove through the wrought-iron gates, it was as if nothing had happened. The musicians were in place and the various stations were set up.

The sun's rays warmed a crowd that was well overdue for a sunny day, and people immediately got into the spirit, making the most of their time outdoors. Families picnicked on the grounds, and a younger partying crowd wandered around sampling the food and various wines. They were spending money on wine, which was a good thing.

Feeling immensely proud, Hudson and Jon wove their way through the toga-clad servers, meeting and greeting people. They handed out newsletters and distributed brochures. Jon after a while called it quits, excusing himself to go hear Dara play violin in the tasting tent.

Hudson was fully expecting to run into Talia Chisolm at some point. She'd been too quiet lately.

The thought of that encounter dampened his mood a bit. Refusing to think further about the aggressive Mrs. Chisolm, he went in search of Laila.

"Mr. Godfrey?"

An attractive African-American woman stepped directly into his path, brandishing a card. This must be his first official complaint.

"Fern Williams with the *Seattle Times*. May I have a word with you?" She flashed a laminated badge.

Hudson examined her credentials closely, his stomach clenching and unclenching. Just what he needed, a hungry reporter looking to dig up dirt. She was probably one of those overzealous types who checked the police blotters looking for newsworthy items and had found out about the vandalism, or why else would she be here?

But some publicity was better than none at all. The winery could definitely use a mention in the paper. Maybe they'd even pick up a customer or two.

"Why don't we go into my office where it's quieter and we can talk?" Hudson suggested.

Fern fell in step with him. He offered her a glass of wine but she opted for water instead. Smart of her, she probably wanted to stay sharp and focused.

In his office, Fern uncapped her bottle and slid into the chair across from him. She crossed long legs at the ankle and patted her blunt cut in place.

Hudson found himself comparing her to Laila. No contest as far as he was concerned.

The reporter was pretty in a too-perfect way. Her hair didn't move and her makeup looked as if an artist had painted a palette on her face. Her polished nails were obviously professionally done but he doubted they were hers.

Hudson much preferred the fresh, natural look. He liked the kind of woman who looked as if she wouldn't mind her hair being messed up, and might even consider going hiking or jogging. He liked women whose looks didn't surprise you the morning after—women like Laila.

Forget her for a moment; he needed to focus on this interview.

"What is it you'd like to know?" Hudson asked Fern.

She smiled and Hudson swore those teeth were veneers.

"I've been reading up on you and your partner," she said, shifting in her seat. "I'm intrigued. Do you mind if I record our conversation." Fern removed a tiny recorder from the expensive purse she'd placed on the floor beside her.

"Actually, I do mind."

The recorder was quickly tucked back in her purse.

"Why are you so intrigued?" Hudson asked. "Washington is full of young entrepreneurs, people who are worth billions simply by taking a risk."

Fern pressed her lips together, smoothing out her lipstick.

"I do wonder why two attorneys, graduates of an excellent university, would start a business few African-Americans have ventured into. You're employee-friendly and offer frontline benefits. You even grow some of your own grapes. This wasn't a family business you inherited. What is it about grape growing that appealed to you?"

Fern's line of questioning was not what Hudson had anticipated. She seemed sympathetic and on his side. He relaxed and began letting down his guard. If Fern was looking for a human interest story he could give her one. The *Seattle Times* wasn't exactly a neighborhood rag. It had wide distribution.

Hudson recounted the tale of him and Jon meeting in law school while getting their JD's, and how one night they concluded that wasn't enough for them. They'd both been on the same page, wanting to create a legacy that could be passed on to their families.

"Why wine?" Fern probed. "What did you know about the manufacturing process?" She waited, staring at him through heavily mascared eyelashes, daring him to look away.

Hudson chose his words carefully.

"Jon and I knew squat about wine, except for enjoying a glass or two. We researched, spoke to people and decided to give it a try."

"You went into a business you knew very little about, hoping it would be profitable?" She sounded like she didn't believe him.

"We did our research and picked up the land and building at a reasonable price. That was way before living in Woodinville became fashionable."

Fern scribbled on a pad. "Any regrets?"

"Of course we wish we could make a zillion dollars yesterday."

"Don't we all?"

Fern leaned in, and a whiff of her expensive perfume hit him square in the nose. He tried not to stare at her cleavage visible through the gaping shirt.

Her tone was neutral and without inflection when she asked, "What's this I hear about possible sabotage?"

"I'm not sure I understand you."

Although Fern's gaze locked with his, her pen remained poised.

"There's been a series of mishaps on the property. You've had labor problems, an accident, fire, and most recently you've been vandalized."

Be careful now. Answer a question with a question.

Hudson's caution buttons went way back on high. "What would make you think it was sabotage?" he asked.

"Well it seems awfully suspicious to me. Here

are two African-American vintners, probably the only ones around for miles. Maybe the only ones in existence. You're an easy target."

"Why?"

It was clear as crystal to Hudson where Fern was heading, and he was not about to walk into that trap. He'd never been the type to blame his woes on race, nor did he subscribe to the victim mentality.

Fern was waiting for an answer.

"What don't you understand? Do I have to spell it out for you?" she asked.

"Yes, please. I'd like to make sure I'm answering your question."

"Someone obviously has a problem with two black men being in this business. They're determined to see you fail," she said, convincingly.

Hudson laughed dismissively, although the last thing he felt like doing was laughing.

"In that case I wish I knew who that someone was. I'm going to need to get back out there shortly. Are we almost done?"

"Just a couple of more questions. What's your vision for Jon Hudson? Where do you want to be in five years?"

This was more in line with the types of questions he'd expected.

"Jon and I want to make a mark on this industry," Hudson said honestly. "Not only do we want to sell wine, but we want to educate the consumer. We believe wine drinking should be an event, and we want to introduce wines to the mainstream. Good wines don't have to be expensive. Our goal is to manufacture and bottle wines appealing to every palate and wallet."

Fern uncrossed her legs and placed them firmly on the ground. She slapped her business card on his desk.

"That's noble of you, Hudson. Now let's just cut to the chase." She leaned in even further, giving him an eyeful of cleavage. "You can be straight with me. How about having dinner with me later. I'll be expecting your call."

Hudson sat stunned as Fern breezed out. The conversation had taken a most unexpected turn. One he wasn't sure he liked.

Chapter 19

"Have you seen Hudson?" Laila asked Barbara Manson when she spotted the tasting-room manager coming from the main building.

Laila guessed the woman had needed a brief respite from the crowds, and crowded it certainly was out there. By the afternoon, revelers had come out in full force. Many had gotten into the spirit of things and arrived wearing togas. Some even carried grapes and harps in hand.

Barb jutted a finger in the direction of the Victorian house that served as the main building.

"Hudson's in his office behind closed doors. Is there a problem?"

Laila shook her head. "Nothing I can't handle. I did want to run something by him, though."

A man brushed by her almost knocking her over. He was carrying a shopping bag. Barbara called to him.

"Hold up a minute, Luis, I've got something for you to do."

He darted a frantic look at Barbara and continued on his way, shouting over his shoulder, "The boss, he asked me to do something for him already. I have to go."

Still casting furtive glances over his shoulder as if expecting Barb to chase him, he raced away.

Barb shrugged. "Oh, well. He must be in a hurry to get somewhere. Your friend the violinist is doing an awesome job in the tasting tent." She prepared to sprint off in the other direction. "Most of the men listening to her are totally captivated and so is our boss."

"You're speaking of Jon, I suppose. Yes, Dara is very talented. I'm glad to hear that she's being appreciated."

Laila needed to bring to Hudson's attention a group of young people just on the brink of getting drunk. She suspected they were under the age of twenty-one and must have presented false identification to get in. She'd tried finding Jon but was told he'd gone off on an errand.

Waving to Barb she entered the main building where a small group of visitors were being given a tour of the facility. She acknowledged the tour guide and continued on her way.

"Hi, Steven."

Laila was about to tap on Hudson's closed door when it flew open and a woman sauntered through.

"I'm looking forward to seeing you later," she tossed over her shoulder. "Nine is good for me. We can eat late, European-style."

"Pardon me," Laila said as the woman whizzed by, almost running her over.

Hudson remained seated behind his desk in something of a daze.

"Is this bad timing?" Laila asked, feeling as if a vise had just been placed around her heart.

"No, no, come in. Is there something wrong?"

Hudson sounded distracted and dreamy as if he wasn't quite with her. Laila wondered what he was doing behind closed doors when literally hundreds of people were running around on his property, sampling his wines.

She stood in front of him trying not to let his good looks distract her, and ignoring the musky soapy scent she'd come to associate with him.

"I'm here to give you a heads-up on a potential problem," she said.

That got his full attention.

"I don't think I can handle another issue today." He clasped his hands behind his head and waited for her to go on. "I've already dealt with someone slipping and falling. Thankfully it was just a minor scrape and nothing as serious as a broken bone. We've also run out of stemware and had to resort to using plastic cups. Anyone who knows anything about good wine knows plastic changes the taste. And just a few minutes ago one of the mimes I hired had to be sent home. The man overdosed on his own body paint, can you believe it?"

Poor Hudson sounded as if he'd had it. He was stressed to the max and not finding humor in any of this.

"I'm sorry to be the bearer of more bad news," Laila said. "But there's a group of rowdy kids being disruptive. When I left they were heckling the harpist. They look underage to me, and I think they might have spent too much time in the tasting room."

Hudson's brows furrowed.

"Are you telling me they're drunk?"

"I'd say they were on their way."

An expletive followed as he catapulted out of his chair.

"That's just what we need. I better put an end to it before things get really out of hand. Security's supposed to be handling these kinds of issues and that's what I'm paying them for. We'll take the golf cart. It's quicker."

He'd made the assumption that she would go with him, and of course she would, although she was still wondering what exactly had transpired between him and the woman who'd blown past her without so much as a word.

When they arrived at the spot where Laila had last seen the group, the teenagers were nowhere to be found. After circling the property a couple of times she almost gave up.

"Let's just park the cart and check out the tasting tent," Laila suggested.

"Good idea."

Things had picked up inside and it was close to being a mob scene. Long lines of people waited to make purchases, wine bottles in hand. A three-piece jazz ensemble had replaced Dara, and Laila's friend was nowhere to be seen. Laila suspected she knew with whom she was passing time.

"That's them," Laila said, pointing to a group of young people on the makeshift dance floor wildly gyrating.

Hudson headed off in the direction of the security guard standing at the entrance of the tent. She was unable to hear the exchange, but the man had a face like a lemon by the time he approached the young revelers. He escorted them out to loud applause.

"That should never have happened," Hudson grumbled when he returned. "I instructed the servers to refuse service to anyone they suspect is underage or even looks close to intoxication. I expected a few to slip through the cracks, but security should have been on top of things. Where's Jon, I wonder?"

Laila explained that she'd been told Jon had gone off to run an errand. Her guess was that he'd taken Dara with him.

"So how do you think our soiree is going over so far?" he asked, scanning the area for potential problems.

"All in all it seems to be going very well. The food stations are getting a lot of action. It's good exposure for the restaurants that donated food. Wine sales also look very promising and everyone seems to be having a good time. What more can you ask?"

Hudson squeezed her hand before bringing it to his lips.

"Then in that case we shouldn't let this good music go to waste. Let's dance."

"I thought you'd never ask."

They retraced their steps and entered the tasting tent. By then the jazz ensemble had stepped things up a bit and were playing a lively tune. The more mature guests were on the floor two-stepping.

Laila was swept into Hudson's arms. One hand clutched his shoulder and the other the hand he held out. They silently counted out the beat before he moved off. Hudson was easy to follow and that might well have something to do with them being used to each other. Laila had never mastered the intricacies of a fox-trot but she was a good faker.

A voice came at them over the music.

"Can we have a loud round of applause for Hudson Godfrey, one of the owners of Jon Hudson Cellars? That's him on the dance floor."

The applause following was deafening. Laila was pleased that Hudson had been publicly recognized. All that hard work had earned him an ovation.

"Speech, speech," someone chanted. Soon the whole room took up the chant.

"You'd better get up there," Laila said, nudging Hudson to the front of the room.

He accepted the mike and waited for the room to quiet. Laila stood off to the side, assessing the mixed bag of people. Everyone seemed to be having a good time. Servers moved effortlessly around, trays held high, stopping to offer tastes of the various blends to anyone so desiring.

The blending station had turned out to be the "it" place to be. A long line of people were now waiting to pay, bottles in hand. Who would have thought to get more cash registers? Perhaps she should start another line for those paying by check or having exact change.

Laila's gaze landed on one of the men cleaning up the tables. He was familiar looking and she was certain she knew him from somewhere. It was the same man she'd passed earlier when she'd been on her way to find Hudson. It was Luis, and a nervous

Luis at that, judging by the way he cast furtive glances over his shoulder.

Maybe she was making way too much of it. Laila listened intently as Hudson spoke. He was thanking everyone for coming out and asking them to be sure to let him know which wines they liked best. Jon and Dara had appeared from somewhere and stood hand in hand.

"I'd say our party is a big hit," Laila said, greeting them.

"Yes, cars are double- and triple-parked all the way up the driveway, and people are lined up to come in. Everyone I've run into seems happy," Jon said.

"And they're buying," Laila added. "I'd hate for people to put back bottles because the lines are moving too slow. I was thinking of opening another line for those with exact change or cash."

"Do what you need to do. Dara and I will help. Won't we, Dara?"

"Of course."

Dara looked like she would do just about anything Jon asked of her. The two had clearly clicked, and for a brief moment Laila envied her.

Staying busy was one way to keep her mind off Hudson, a man she couldn't have.

Laila approached Luis bussing the tables and asked him if he minded moving one of them against the wall. His forehead was coated in perspiration, which was strange given it wasn't exactly hot in there. He appeared jumpy and on edge. Hudson spotted Jon and called him up to the microphone.

Laila tried getting their attention. She wanted them to announce another payment line had opened. Finally she caught Jon's eye and he made the announcement.

He'd barely gotten the words out of his mouth when a line began forming in front of her. For the next half hour she and Dara were kept busy. The men had attracted a fan club of mostly women whose questions ran the gamut from the intelligent to the inane.

Out of the corner of her eye, Laila spotted Luis fumbling around in the garbage. Something about the man's jerky movements and darted looks put her on the alert.

"Dara, can you handle ringing up this merchandise on your own for a moment?" she said to her friend.

"Of course."

Pretending to head for a Porta Potti she ambled up to the man.

"Luis," Laila called, "have you lost something?"

He jumped a mile high, clutching his chest with both hands.

"Oh, miss, you scared me. A guest says she throw out a bag with purchases by accident. I look for it."

Why didn't she believe him?

"Wouldn't it be easier to pick up the entire trash can and take it someplace you can sort through?"

"Yes, ma'am, you are right."

Yet he made no effort to do that. He stood there waiting for her to move along.

"On second thought, you have a lot to do here so why don't I do it for you?" Laila suggested, more to gauge his reaction than anything else.

Luis clutched the trashcan as if it were a lifeline. "Oh, no, ma'am, I can't have you do that. This is my job."

Hudson's voice came from over Laila's shoulder. "Luis, what are you doing here?"

The worker looked like he was about to lose his lunch any moment.

"I-I w-w-was told to come over to this area and help clean up."

"By who?" Jon asked, joining Hudson.

"My boss." Luis pointed a finger in a vague direction. He assumed a protective stance in front of the waste receptacle.

"Okay, in that case, you may carry on." This came from Hudson.

Laila noted again that Luis was making no effort to continue to sift through the debris. She decided to keep an eye on him. Something didn't seem right.

She continued on her way toward the nearest Porta Potti while Hudson and Jon continued to circulate. She doubled back, coming up on Luis from another direction. She noticed the small shopping bag in his hand. It was the same one he'd had during their earlier encounter when he'd run away from her and Barb Manson.

Laila tapped Luis on the shoulder. Again he overreacted, jumping inches into the air. A thin sheen of sweat still coated his forehead and now it rimmed his upper lip.

"I see you found it," Laila said, her eye on the small shopping bag.

"Uh, yes. I must take it to the guest who lost it."

"Why don't I do that for you?" Her fingers curled around the bag's handles but Luis kept a firm grip on his booty. Laila continued to tug. For the next few seconds a tug-of-war ensued. Laila was now determined to gain possession of the bag and its contents.

"Point out the guest and I'll take it to them," she said in a firm voice.

When Luis scanned the surrounding area, she gave one final tug. The handle of the bag broke and a can inside rolled across the ground. Luis charged through the crowd as if there were dogs at his heels. A guest retrieved the can and handed it to Laila. The man laughed uncontrollably.

"If you wanted us to leave you could have asked nicely," he said.

"I'm sorry."

"That's Liquid Arse you have," he said, pointing to the can. "The equivalent of a stink bomb."

"Liquid what?"

"It makes anywhere smell like the plumbing is broken. One spritz can clear a whole room almost immediately."

Laila examined the can. She thanked the man, thinking the whole situation was getting stranger and stranger. Why would an employee be carrying a can of Liquid Arse around?

Unless…it was too disturbing a thought. She needed to find Hudson and quick.

Chapter 20

"A special occasion deserves a special wine," Hudson announced, pouring one of the special blends into Jon's wineglass.

"I'll drink to that," his partner said, clinking his glass against Hudson's.

They'd retreated briefly to Jon's office, supposedly on the pretense of getting money from the safe. In reality they needed a breather. It was the first time they would actually get a chance to talk.

"We pulled it off. Don't ask me how we did it," Hudson said, gulping a big mouthful of wine, his first taste of alcohol all day.

"And beautifully I might add. Everyone's been

very complimentary and the cash registers have been singing a lively tune. Cha-ching. Now all we need is the press to give us a favorable write-up, and we're set."

Hudson's hands clasped his head. He groaned. "I still haven't made up my mind what to do about Fern Williams."

Jon shot him a puzzled look. "Who's she?"

"A reporter from the *Seattle Times*. You weren't around when she asked to interview the owners."

One of Jon's eyebrows rose. "And you're thinking she might not talk up Jon Hudson Cellars."

"Honestly, I don't know. The interview went well, but at the conclusion she asked me to dinner."

Jon finished his wine and set down his glass. "Any reason you wouldn't go?"

"She wants to have dinner tonight. That's impossible."

"Why?"

"I'm not interested in the woman and we're busy."

"And she's interested in you, and she's a reporter and you could use that to your advantage."

"How so?" Hudson asked, curious to hear how his partner would handle his dilemma.

"I'd go and have dinner with her, but I'd keep things strictly professional. We might get a good write-up out of it."

A loud banging interrupted the conversation. The men exchanged looks.

"Yes?" Hudson called.

"It's Laila and Dara. We need you."

Something about Laila's tone made Hudson catapult out of his chair and open the door. Laila entered the room with Dara trailing her. In Laila's hand she held a paper bag that had seen better days.

"Sorry to interrupt," she said, "but you need to know about this."

"What's going on?" Jon asked, sidling up next to the violinist as if he couldn't get enough of her. Although the two didn't touch, the chemistry was palpable.

Laila recounted running into Luis earlier and his bizarre behavior. She offered up the can of Liquid Arse as proof he was up to no good.

"When we tried to question Luis he went racing off like a bat out of hell," she said. "It was disturbing."

Hudson took the can from her, turning it this way and that. He read the ingredients out loud.

"Hmmmm, isn't hydrogen sulfide the stuff that stinks?"

"Yes, smells like rotten eggs," his partner supplied.

"That's exactly why I'm not buying Luis's story that a guest tossed the bag out by mistake," Laila restated.

Hudson steepled his fingers. "I suppose it could be possible."

"Something smells off to me," Jon joked, trying to add some levity to the situation.

When no one laughed he grew serious again.

"Why, though? What would prompt this kind of behavior?"

"It could have been disastrous. Can you imagine the stampede with all those people bailing?" Laila said. "Guests could have gotten hurt and the business would have gone right down the toilet, no pun intended."

"Can you imagine the kind of press the winery would have gotten?" Dara added, shuddering.

Jon rolled his eyes. "I don't want to think of it. Publicity like that we don't need." He gave Dara a big bear hug. "I'm going to try to find Scott and see what he knows about this guy. Want to come with me?"

She took his arm and they hustled off.

After they left, Hudson said, "Luis was the man who came to find me when there was that labor uprising."

"I'm fairly certain he is. He seemed like a straight-up guy, loyal and concerned, which is why this is even more perplexing."

"Maybe it's all a misunderstanding. If so, Jon will get to the bottom of it." Hudson glanced at his watch. "Half an hour to our official closing time, better get out there. I need to scout around and find that reporter, Fern Williams. She and I have dinner plans."

How insulting to be dismissed like that especially after all she'd done to make this weekend work. Men were such insensitive jerks at times. Hudson clearly was hot for the *Seattle Times* reporter and he wasn't even trying to cover that up. When would she get it through that thick skull of hers they were over?

Laila stayed busy helping Barb Manson inventory the remaining bottles of wine. The tasting tent had done a brisk business all day and there were discarded wineglasses and barely nibbled-on plates of food all over the place. The servers were picking up as best as they could while a few tipsy guests swayed on the dance floor.

Dara was nowhere to be found. She'd deserted them for Jon. The steam coming off the two rivaled any boiling kettle. Laila already had the feeling she would not be seeing much of the violinist this weekend. She was tempted to leave her a note and catch the next ferry back to Whidbey, but a promise was a promise, and she'd agreed to help Hudson out for the entire weekend. She meant to keep her word.

Laila heard Mariner's joyous woofs as he frolicked with the other dogs. Oh, to be without a care in the world, your only concern being when your next meal would be out. Animal-friendly as Washington was, many people had brought their dogs with them. They'd let them roam free while they toured the winery and sampled what Jon Hudson Cellars had to offer.

As the afternoon progressed, Laila was glad she'd declined Hudson's offer to be his guest. She'd accepted his counteroffer to stay at one of the hotels where the winery had a business arrangement. Lucky for her it was also an animal-friendly property, which meant she could keep Mariner.

In retrospect, and given what had transpired less than a half hour ago, someone had been looking out for her. How embarrassing to be staying at Hudson's place when he had a dinner date, and one he was so obviously looking forward to?

Barb shoved the last bottle back in its carton and hefted it onto her shoulder.

"What are your plans for dinner? You and I need to find somewhere to party," she said, picking up on Laila's mood.

"There's a good dose of room service in store for me," Laila answered, forcing lightness into her voice.

"Not room service. Yuck. We need to celebrate, and I've got just the restaurant. Knowing it would be a busy weekend I've already made reservations."

Barb's invitation sounded like a better option than spending the night holed up in some hotel room, muttering to herself. From the very beginning, Laila had liked the woman, and dinner was a good opportunity to get to know her better.

As they were leaving, Laila caught a glimpse of Hudson helping Fern Williams into the Infiniti. The reporter tossed back streaked extensions and laughed into his face. The sight of them put Laila's teeth on edge. Hudson had made his choice and it clearly wasn't her.

The restaurant Barb chose was a dog-friendly one, and dogs were welcome to lie out on the patio or remain out front. Laila had considered making a quick stop and leaving Mariner back in the room, but she didn't want to risk him howling and disturbing other guests.

The Mountain Top, the chosen restaurant, had a casual but chic ambience and great mountain views. Judging by the line waiting to get in, it was a good thing they had reservations. Soon they were shown to a table on the outside patio.

Wooed by the roaring fires that provided both ambience and warmth, Mariner made himself comfortable. A delicious hickory smell tickled Laila's nostrils. She sank gratefully into one of the wooden deck chairs and placed her feet on the matching ottoman.

"Sitting feels good," she said, rotating her ankles. "I must have walked miles today."

"Me, too," Barb said, joining her. "The good thing is that all of that lifting and carrying builds muscle."

"Did Luis ever surface again?"

Laila picked up her water and sipped on it. She nibbled on a bread stick she'd dug out of the basket.

Barb shook her head. "No one's seen him since he took off like a bat out of hell from the tasting room. The whole thing is strange if you ask me. I wonder if a background check was done on him?"

"I'm not sure if that's Jon Hudson's policy."

The topic changed. Laila was curious about why Barb had chosen a traditionally male career. When the meal was served the conversation focused on Laila.

"I heard that you swapped your home to come to Washington State," Barb blurted.

"It was a houseboat actually."

"That was brave of you to open your home to a stranger. Do you miss it?"

"I miss the sun at times, but the cottage—actually more like a carriage house—that I live in is really quite nice."

"I don't know if I'd want some strange person in my house, touching my things, using my bathroom, invading my space."

Laila lined up her knife and fork neatly.

"I considered all of that but I needed a change."

Barb eyed her from under long lashes.

"I hope you don't mind me saying this, because it's actually none of my business. It's been floating around that you're involved with Hudson. Supposedly you came to Washington State to try to work things out with him."

The rumor mill was already all over it. She should have known. Mariner, with his keen hearing, having heard Hudson's name, began whimpering.

"Hudson and I are no longer involved," Laila said carefully. She liked Barb, but she didn't know her that well, and saw no reason to share the details of her and Hudson's relationship.

Laila had to strain to hear Barb's response.

"Good, I'm glad you guys are no longer an item because Hudson is here with a woman hanging all over him. It might be a business dinner, but it sure doesn't look like it to me."

Laila refused to crane her neck or change her facial expressions. Of all the restaurants in Woodinville why did Hudson have to pick this one? Was he taunting her? She risked a glance in the direction Barb was staring. What a huge mistake that was.

The same attractive woman she'd seen getting into his car had her arm hooked through his. She was hanging on to him as if he were her lifeline. Her head was very close to his as if they shared some intimate secret. Hudson seemed to be loving the attention. He was grinning from ear to ear and looking at Fern Williams as if she were one of the bottles from his private collection.

"Well that's one way to ensure the winery gets a good write-up," Barb said lightly.

"What do you mean?"

"Come on now. Everyone's heard of Fern Williams. Her restaurant reviews can make or break a place. Fern is sort of like Oprah. She gives you a mention and you're an instant success."

"Are you suggesting Hudson is using Fern?" Laila asked, curious.

"Now did I say that?"

Laila's loyalty kicked in. Upset as she was with Hudson, fair was fair.

"Hudson's not a user. He seems to be enjoying Fern's company. He certainly doesn't look like he wants to run away."

He might have used you, an ugly voice said.

She would not let negativity creep in.

"Whatever," Barb said, not picking up on Laila's rapidly deteriorating mood. "It was a mighty smart move to invite her out. I have my mind set on dessert, how about you?"

Dessert was the last thing on Laila's mind now. Why stay and prolong the agony of seeing Hudson with someone he obviously enjoyed?

But Barb didn't seem in a hurry to leave. She'd been good company so far and a welcome distraction. It seemed a shame to cut short the evening of a woman who'd been very kind. If Laila returned to the hotel she'd spend the rest of the evening stewing.

"No dessert for me," she said as the server

hovered. "I'll have a cup of tea and watch you eat dessert." She yawned, signaling it wouldn't be a very late night. "I'm starting to fade."

"Then why don't we leave?" Barb signaled to the server for the check.

Mariner, who'd been sniffing, circling and whining, bolted across the patio toward Hudson.

"Mariner, Mariner, come back here," Laila shouted, taking off right after him. Every eye in the place was now on them.

The canine, usually good on command, totally ignored her. He'd found Hudson and was in la-la land when Hudson began scratching him behind the ears. Hudson's companion didn't look exactly enchanted by the new arrival. The last thing she wanted was to be upstaged by a slobbering dog.

"I'm sorry," Laila said, hooking two fingers through her dog's collar and trying to steer him away. She studiously avoided looking at Hudson. Seeing him with another woman was like being stabbed. There was no way to describe the pain knifing through her heart.

She couldn't possibly compete with a well-put-together woman like Fern Williams. Not the way she looked in her swirling ankle-length skirt, shirt tied at the waist, and sweater draped over her shoulders. Next to Fern she was a dried-up old matron. The chic reporter wore Donna Karan from head to hem, and those shoes had to be Via Spiga.

"Don't run off," Hudson said. "Come meet Fern Williams. Sit and stay awhile."

Was he out of his mind? Did he really think that she was going to join him and her replacement?

Laila gestured vaguely in the direction she'd just come from.

"Thank you but I'm having dinner with Barb, and we're just about to leave."

"Then have her join us, as well."

Why? So Barb could be there to witness her humiliation as she was forced to smile and pretend she wasn't shattered?

She went through the motions of shaking Fern's hand. The reporter's stare was cold and unyielding. She looked Laila over and dismissed her as not worth her time.

"It's nice of you to invite us, but we were just leaving," Laila insisted.

To her surprise Hudson shoved his chair back and strode across the restaurant, heading for where Barb was seated. Laila was left with her fingers hooked through Mariner's collar, facing a seething Fern Williams.

"So much for a nice, quiet dinner," Fern fumed.

"I'm sorry my dog disturbed your dinner," Laila said.

"I'm sorry you did, too."

What a rude, ungracious woman. How could Hudson stomach her?

Thankfully Barb and Hudson were now on their way back.

"I told Hudson we were just leaving," Barb said, cool as ever. "He insisted on picking up our tab and having us join him."

"Hudson, that really wasn't necessary. Barb and I were going to split dinner," Laila protested.

"Too late. It's already done." Hudson held out two chairs for them.

They sat. Hudson held up his end of the conversation while a sullen Fern grunted, pretending to be engaged. Having no choice, Laila ordered the tea that she'd been considering while Barb indulged in a sinful dessert: a concoction of chocolate, strawberries and cream. After a suitable time had elapsed, the two women sent silent signals to each other and stood.

"Thank you. It's been really enjoyable, but we need to get going," Barb said. She looked as if she was reluctant to cut their evening short.

"I wish you'd both stay longer, but at least allow me to walk you to your car," Hudson offered. Fern's tight-lipped grin barely contained her displeasure.

"There really is no need to," Laila protested, getting a firm hold on Mariner and practically pulling the reluctant dog from the restaurant.

"Ah, but there is."

Draping an arm around them both, Hudson walked them out.

Seated in Barb's truck she exhaled a long held breath.

"Wow! Was that ever awkward," Barb said.

Laila was in complete agreement. After all she'd been through, she wanted to go to her bed and wallow in her misery. But she'd committed to helping out for the entire weekend and there was still tomorrow to get through.

"Know what I think?" Barb said, glancing back to make sure Mariner, in the bed of her monster truck, was seated. "I don't think Hudson is over you."

"Nonsense."

"I've seen the way he looks at you when he thinks no one else is looking."

"And how is that?"

"Like he wants to devour you."

"You're mistaken," Laila mumbled, hoping that she wasn't.

"I assure you I am not."

Chapter 21

Laila's Blog
Sunday, April 1

Seeing Hudson with that reporter, Fern Williams, almost made me lose it, and just when I'd determined Talia Chisolm wasn't anyone to worry about. It was Hudson who'd forced us to join them, but he was probably just being polite. He couldn't exactly ignore two of his employees.

But seeing them together was tough. I'd had a hard time going to bed after that. I'd tossed and turned all night speculating about what their rela-

tionship might be. When morning rolled around I was sick to my stomach. In my head I could clearly hear wedding bells chiming for those two.

Mariner sensed my mood and circled and circled. He licked my hands sympathetically. I focused on pleasanter things like the royalties I would get if sales continued the way they were. I would be this much closer to funding my scholarship for a deserving copywriter. I've got to get up and let out my dog.

With a forced sense of cheeriness, Laila made it through the remainder of the weekend. Sunday brought an entirely different crowd to Jon Hudson Cellars: a spending crowd out to enjoy more of the precious sun. Laila had seen Hudson from a distance, but other than nodding at each other, there hadn't been time to talk.

She kept herself busy, circulating among the guests and helping Barb with whatever needed to be done. There wasn't even Dara to talk to. Her friend had shown up the following morning looking as if she'd won the coveted Award of Excellence from *Wine Spectator.* No reason to ask who she'd been with last night. Her smile said it all.

By the time close of business rolled around, Laila was more than ready to go home. She said her goodbyes to the staff and other contracted workers and looked around for Hudson. Dara had already told her she'd be staying on an extra day and that she and Jon planned on taking a short road trip to get to know each other.

There was no Hudson to be found, and Jon and Dara had left on their minivacation already. The prudent thing was to leave Hudson a note that she was taking off.

With some trepidation Laila entered his office, found a pad and pen and scribbled a note. Mariner was still romping with the other dogs when she called him and leashed him.

By the time she arrived at the cottage, she was slowly decompressing. She'd never thought she'd be so happy to see her home, albeit a borrowed one. Laila lit a fire and wandered around reorienting herself. She admired Brock's paintings and touched some of his cherished antique pieces. The familiarity of home brought with it a strange sense of comfort. She felt as if she'd been gone for months and it was good to be back in familiar surroundings.

Something told her to check the answering machine. A blinking light indicated unplayed messages. She listened, determined to deal with it all tomorrow. Con was looking for her, several of her clients were expecting call backs and someone from the Whidbey Island Copywriting Association left a message informing her of the next meeting.

Laila's heart lodged in her throat when she heard Brock Lawrence's voice. This was the third time he'd called since they'd done a house swap. Something must be up.

Anticipating something awful, Laila picked up the landline and punched in the number to Brock's cell phone. From the moment he answered, she knew something was wrong.

"Please, no more bad news."

"Brock, this is Laila Stewart. I'm not sure when you called me. I've been away for a few days and just got back. What's going on?"

She heard Brock's sharp intake of breath and braced herself for problems.

"I tried you on your cell but for whatever reason the calls weren't getting through. I hate to do this to you, but I'm going to have to cut my stay in Fort Lauderdale short."

This wasn't at all what she'd expected. Laila's mind was racing, already thinking about what this meant for her.

"When are you looking at heading back?" she asked, already dreading his answer.

"In the next day or two. Technically I should be in Washington State right now. My ex called to let me know my daughter was in a car accident and it was serious."

"Oh, Brock, I'm so sorry. How is she doing?"

"Shelli has a broken arm, leg and ruptured spleen."

"That's awful."

Brock filled her in on the details.

"She's holding her own but I'm worried sick and feel I need to get home and see for myself how she's doing."

"Of course you do. I'd expect that of you."

What kind of father would Brock be if he didn't fly home to be with his daughter? It didn't leave Laila much time to pack up her things and prepare for the cross-country trek, but maybe it came at an opportune time.

She'd have to try reaching the friends she'd made to say goodbye, and she couldn't help feeling as if she was leaving unfinished business behind. Perhaps it was prompted by Barbara Manson's comments, because although Laila had dismissed the woman's observations about Hudson, deep down she'd hoped she was right.

"I really am sorry," Brock said, breaking into Laila's thoughts. "Under other circumstances I would fly in for a few days, stay at a hotel and then leave, but due to my daughter's extensive injuries I think I need to be around for a while."

"No problem."

Laila empathized with him some more, and they discussed where to leave their respective keys. She used the next couple of hours to begin packing up and to start the arduous business of cleaning. Then she tried Con. When he didn't answer, she felt an enormous sense of relief and left a message.

She was wrung out. Early tomorrow she would

try Dara, Hudson or Jon to let them know what was going on, then later that same day she would start the drive back. It would be impossible to find a professional car mover who would pick up a vehicle on twenty-four-hour notice and that left her no choice but to drive her own car.

She was sorry Brock's daughter had been injured, but in some ways the timing couldn't be better. She was falling for Hudson all over again and in a major way.

And she needed to nip that in the bud, and quickly.

Hudson's jaw clenched and unclenched as he listened to the message left on his voice mail. It was the last thing he'd expected. His instincts told him to pick up the phone and try to convince Laila to stay. She could come and live with him until she found a place of her own. On the other hand that might not be a smart move.

As he deliberated, Jon came sauntering into his office.

"You look like you've just heard some really bad news," his partner said.

"I have."

Hudson put the phone on speaker and replayed Laila's message.

"Seems rather sudden don't you think?" Hudson said.

"Well, you usually don't plan an accident."

"Yes, I know, but she's leaving us in the lurch, right when things are starting to pick up. We can really use her help. What does Dara say?"

Jon shrugged. "I haven't talked to her, not since she headed back for Langley early this morning." He slapped his hands on Hudson's desk and leaned in. "So what are you going to do about the woman, bro? Let her get away again?"

Hudson snorted. "I'm not ready to make a commitment. We're this close to getting our business off the ground. Once the official release happens and orders really start coming in, I can give some thought to a personal life."

"It may be too late by then, but you know best." Jon hesitated and then decided just to go for it. "Laila made the first move coming all the way out here. The ball is in your court now, dude. Fumble and you may lose it forever."

"Look, you and I have completely different approaches to relationships. I like to make sure everything's set up nicely before I do my slam dunk. You on the other hand get handed the ball and you run with it."

Jon smiled at his partner. "I play to win, bro. I'm all for seizing the moment. Deep in your gut you know what's right."

Jon's words had merit to them, but it wasn't as if they were talking years here, just another month or so to make sure the business was stable.

"I'll give Dara a jingle later and see what she knows," Jon offered, preparing to take off. "Have you seen the nice write-up Fern Williams gave us?"

"No, I haven't," Hudson said.

"Jessie was reading a copy of the *Seattle Times* when I came in. Should I ask her to bring it in?"

"Sure."

Shortly after his partner left, Jessie stuck her head in the open doorway.

"You wanted to see this?" she asked, waving the paper at him. "I have several copies. Yours is in your in-box."

Hudson hadn't even looked. He'd been much too distracted by Laila's message.

"By the way," Jessie added. "Fern Williams is looking for you. She's already left several messages and so has Talia Chisolm."

Hudson couldn't stop himself from groaning. After Jessie diplomatically retreated, he picked up the newspaper, found Fern's article and read it. She'd said some very nice things about the owners of Jon Hudson, the recent event and the wine itself. Fingers crossed that would bring in orders from major retailers. Ever since the Woodinville weekend, the traffic to the Jon Hudson Cellars' Web site had jumped, and online wine orders had tripled.

He'd deal with Talia first and get her out of the way. But the soon-to-be-divorced Mrs. Chisolm surprised him. She sounded mighty chipper when she greeted him, and he braced himself for the litany of complaints about her husband, Brandon.

"I don't have an update for you," he said, broaching the subject. Brandon Chisolm's attorney had stopped returning Jon's calls.

"Well I have an update for you," Talia said, her laughter tinkling in his ear. Hudson wondered whether she'd been drinking.

He took a wild guess. "You worked out a settlement on your own."

It wouldn't be the first time a client had done that, nor would it be the last.

"We did. Brandon and I are getting back together."

After an acrimonious battle, Brandon must have realized it would be cheaper to keep Talia. Hudson was not at all sorry it worked out the way it did.

"Congratulations! I'm happy for you," he said. "I'll send you a final bill."

"Send it to Brandon. He's picking up all the expenses associated with the divorce proceedings," Talia said breezily. "It was his idea initially. I never wanted a divorce."

She truly was a piece of work.

Hudson wished Talia a happy life and assured her his bill would be sent shortly. Afterward he blew out a relieved breath and picked up the phone again. At least he would no longer have to worry about Talia Chisolm. Brandon would probably settle up quickly and that would mean a nice chunk of income coming in. The business could certainly use the money.

Next up was Fern; after her, he'd call Laila. He'd save the best for last.

To Hudson's relief, Fern Williams was not available when he called. He left a message thanking her for the nice write-up. It would have been great to maintain a professional relationship, but all signals suggested she was looking for something more intimate. Fern was entertaining but way too aggressive for him.

Calling Laila would be next on his list. Hudson closed his door before punching in his ex-girlfriend's number. He went right into voice mail and decided not to leave a message. There were parts of Whidbey Island that had virtually no wireless reception, so that could be the problem. He tried her at her house and when that rang and rang, Hudson left a message on the answering machine.

His intercom buzzed and, still preoccupied, he depressed the button.

"What's up, Jessie?"

"There are two detectives here to see you."

"I'll be right out."

Hudson entered the outer room, where a nervous Jessie feigned interest in her computer monitor. Two of the detectives who'd been involved in the investigation paced. They'd called with periodic updates but no concrete leads.

"What can I do for you, gentlemen?" Hudson asked.

"Can we speak with you privately?" The taller of them asked.

Hudson led the men into his office and gestured to two chairs at his desk.

"Please have a seat."

He remained standing while they folded themselves into the chairs.

"We picked up an employee of yours earlier today," the taller cop began.

"Was this in association with the tent's destruction?"

"It's possible. However, at this point it's believed he might have started the fire."

"Is he a past or present employee?"

"According to the identification he had on him he works for you now."

A muscle in Hudson's jaw twitched—a sure sign that his irritation was slowly building.

"Does this employee have a name?"

Both men exchanged glances. The one who'd been quiet finally spoke up.

"Ever heard of Luis Ortiz?"

"Ortiz? Luis?" Hudson repeated. "Why do you think he started the fire?"

"Remember that gasoline can we found in the garbage?" This came from the shorter one again.

"Yes?"

"Ortiz's fingerprints were all over it. We ran a background check on him and discovered he's an illegal immigrant."

Luis Ortiz? An olive-skinned man approaching middle age; supposedly a loyal employee. Why would he want to put Jon Hudson Cellars out of business? He couldn't think what he'd done to the man.

"Did he say why he did it?" Hudson asked.

"He says he was promised a job with a promotion and raise at another winery."

"Now that's interesting. Who would promise such a thing?"

"Do you have a Scott working for you?"

"I do. Scott Wilkinson?"

"We're here to ask him some questions," the taller detective said.

Hudson was still processing that information when he depressed the intercom's buzzer.

"Jessie, find Scott and have him come here immediately. Also page Jon wherever he is. Make no mention that detectives are here."

"Okay."

While they waited the detectives filled Hudson in on what they knew. Luis Ortiz had been let go from a farm when the owner discovered his illegal status. He'd had some minor run-ins with the law but had been out of trouble for years. It was speculated Scott had somehow found out about Luis's checkered past and threatened to fire Luis if he didn't do exactly as he asked.

"But why would Scott do that?" Hudson said, speaking out loud. "I've been very good to him."

"Scott's Norm Linton's nephew—the owner of Linton Estates. Isn't he the neighboring winery and a competitor of yours?"

The intercom buzzed again.

"Yes, Jessie?" Hudson said.

"Jon's here."

"Send him in."

Jonathan Woods entered. He looked around and quickly assessed the situation. The detectives introduced themselves. Frank was the taller of the two, Steve the shorter.

"You might want to sit," Hudson suggested.

Jonathan declined. Instead he folded his arms and listened as the detectives repeated the story. Halfway through, Jessie stuck her head in the office.

"Scott's here."

"Have him come in," Hudson said.

Scott Wilkinson breezed in as if he didn't have a care in the world. Realizing there was a roomful of people, his entire demeanor changed.

"Did I miss a meeting or something?" he asked.

"Not at all. Have a seat." Jon waved him into a chair.

Scott's eyes darted this way and that before he reluctantly sat.

The detectives flashed their badges and Scott became noticeably startled.

"We'd like to ask you few questions, Scott," Frank said, his voice deceptively low.

Scott shot out of his seat and stood ramrod straight.

"I'm not saying another word without an attorney present."

"Why do you think you need one?" Steve asked. "You're just a person of interest. A person of interest shouldn't need an attorney."

"I know my rights. I have nothing to say." Turning, he exited the room.

"I believe we now have out our number-one suspect," Frank said after Scott Wilkinson left. "You gentlemen need to decide whether you want to press charges or not."

Without hesitation Jon said, "If he turns out to be guilty we'll prosecute to the full extent of the law."

"Damn straight we will," Hudson added.

Chapter 22

Two weeks passed with no word from Hudson.

Laila had decided maybe it was best this way. She'd gone to Washington and gotten her closure. She lay facedown on the grass in the park across the street, arms crossed under her head. The laptop she'd brought with her wasn't open. Ever since leaving Washington State she'd had a hard time concentrating.

Laila had given Mariner a total workout, tossing the Frisbee the dog's way until he got good and tired. Now the worn-out beast sat with his tongue lolling out watching the boats sail by across the way.

The seductive smell of coffee tickled Laila's nostrils. Eyes still closed, she held out her hand.

Kent MacDowell fitted the warm takeout cup into her palm.

"Just what a body needs," Laila murmured, struggling into a seated position so that she could take a sip.

"I'd say that body's held up pretty well given the five- or was it six-day drive from the Pacific Northwest?"

"Six. I took my time but I still feel like a pretzel. It's no fun making that long drive in a VW Beetle with a dog."

"It's no fun making that drive period. Have you heard from your man?"

Hudson was hardly her man, but she wasn't about to argue the point.

"No. I left Hudson a couple of messages but he still hasn't gotten back to me."

"Forget about him. What about his partner?"

"Jon? He's very seriously seeing a friend of mine. He hasn't returned my calls."

"Strange."

"It's not strange. I was useful to them and it was in my interest to help. If their business takes off, I collect royalties."

Kent inhaled a mouthful of coffee, swished it around and then swallowed it.

"You're bitter. I guess I would be the same."

"No, just realistic. I want the winery to be successful so that I can establish a scholarship fund. It's important to me that at least one woman gets a jumpstart on independence. My mother had no one to help her when my father left her."

Laila struggled into an upright position and whistled for Mariner.

Why did Kent have to bring up Hudson's name? Bad enough Hudson hadn't had the decency to return her phone calls, but he'd not even called to inquire if she'd gotten home safely.

So far she'd tried drowning herself in work, catching up on all the copywriting that she'd put on the back burner. For months Jon Hudson Cellars had been her priority. In fact, Hudson had been her priority. But no more.

Kent fell in step beside her, linking his fingers lightly through hers. "For what it's worth, girlfriend, I missed you. That man's a jerk to let you go."

He sounded sincere. She'd missed him, too, and she missed the friends she'd made in Washington; people like Dara, Barb and Con. Con she'd heard from. He still wanted her to write blurbs for the back of his books. She'd give the other two a call before the end of the week.

"I'm taking the boat out later if you'd like to join me," Kent said, leaving her in front of her houseboat.

"I might take you up on that." She waved, watching him walk away.

She'd never considered that Kent might be interested in her. Maybe that's exactly what she needed, a nice little fling.

Hudson was sick to death of being sent off to voice mail hell. He'd left a minimum of two messages on Laila's cell phone with no call back. There was only so much a man could do without sacrificing his pride.

It had been crazy since Laila left. Both Scott Wilkinson and Norm Linton were arrested and now faced trial. Luis Ortiz had sung like a canary, and although Scott had retained an attorney, he'd broken under pressure and said too much.

Scott had ratted out his uncle, who'd given him a monetary bonus to get hired by Jon Hudson Cellars. Scott had been Norm's informant. The vintner was not crazy about having two hotshot African-American entrepreneurs competing against him. He'd hoped to drive them out of business. Several of the men Scott had hired had actually been Linton Estates employees. These had been the rabble-rousers inciting labor issues.

Now that things were finally calming down, Hudson found he was missing Laila like crazy. When Jon stuck his head in his office at the end of the day, Hudson had to ask the question foremost on his mind.

"Has Dara heard from Laila?"

"If she has, she hasn't mentioned it. Have you tried calling her?"

"Yes, several times and I left a couple of messages."

Jon shrugged. ""Did you try the houseboat?"

"No."

Jon was on his way out of Hudson's office when he said over his shoulder, "Why do I feel like I'm dealing with two sophomores in high school? This relationship's become painful to watch. How can two people who love each other keep going around in circles?"

"You think we are?"

"I know that you are. Seize the moment before it's too late and she gets tired of waiting. Get on a plane. Do the right thing by the woman."

"I'm not ready. The winery needs to be on solid ground."

"There'll always be an excuse. Knock me on my head if I make the same mistake with Dara."

After Jon left, Hudson reflected on his partner's words. Did Jon know something he wasn't saying? The winery was so close to finally breaking even. All he needed was a couple of months to see if sales continued to be strong, and then he would make his move.

It would be asking a lot of Laila expecting her to move to Washington permanently. And there was no way he could move to Florida. His business was here.

Hudson scrutinized his desk calendar, circling a couple of dates before pushing the intercom's button.

"Jessie, book me a ticket to Florida," he said, and gave her the dates.

What was wrong with Mariner? Laila's dog had been racing around the houseboat for the last hour, his nonexistent tail twitching, his nose sniffing the air.

"Do you have to go out, boy?" she asked for what had to be at least the sixth time.

She'd even walked him to the door, but that didn't seem to be the issue. He pawed, sniffed, circled and sat down as if expecting someone.

"Okay, okay," she said. "I'll take my laptop upstairs to the garden. You'd like that wouldn't you, boy?"

The dog licked her hand and continued to circle and woof.

His crazed antics made Laila smile, and her mood immediately lightened. She'd been dragging herself through the day and merely going through the motions of living. Something had to change.

Copy Right had always been a wonderful source of happiness but it wasn't enough to own a houseboat, she decided. The work she loved that once gave her such joy couldn't be the beginning and end of it all. There was more to life. Somewhere along the way she'd lost her get-up-and-go, and that needed to change. Blame it on Hudson; no blame it on her.

Balancing a glass of iced tea in one hand and her cell phone and laptop in the other, she followed Mariner up the winding staircase to the rooftop garden. He was still sniffing the air.

Regardless, she was determined to enjoy the lovely April day. She plopped into her favorite deck chair and sat back enjoying the cool ocean breeze. Laila closed her eyes, reflecting on her life. All in all she had it good. She'd accomplished more than most women her age. She had savings, a boat and, God willing, in a few months she'd collect royalties and be able to realize a dream. She could fund a scholarship to help women develop skills.

She'd survive with or without Hudson. It was high time she got into Florida's social scene, and she would start off by accepting Kent's invitation to go sailing.

Mariner continued to circle and sniff the air.

"What's the matter, boy?" Laila asked when he scooted by his favorite lounging area—a potted hibiscus—without even giving it a second look.

Feeling much better, she punched in Kent's number and waited for him to pick up.

"Hey, what time are you planning to take your boat out?" she asked.

"Somewhere around midday. We could do lunch."

The thudding on her front door startled her.

"What the heck…"

Mariner bolted by, almost knocking her over.

"Something the matter?" Kent asked.

"My dog's going nutso. Not sure what's going on. See you in an hour, then."

Mariner was now doing a happy dance as he raced for the stairs. Laila followed closely behind him. He sprinted directly toward the source of the noise and began baying.

"What is the matter with you?"

Mariner hurled himself against the closed door.

"It's only Bob," Laila said, figuring it had to be the mail carrier coming up the gangway.

Anticipating a copywriting package, she threw open the door. She'd offer Bob a cold drink and they'd catch up on the neighborhood news.

"You have a package you need me to sign…uh!"

Laila cupped a hand over her mouth and stared at the man in front of her. Her tongue felt swollen and her fingertips tingled.

"What are you doing here?"

"I came to see you," Hudson said.

Her treacherous dog began slobbering and leaping on Hudson as if he was his sole reason for living. Dog and man did a little jig.

"Come in," Laila finally said, remembering her manners. "Where's your luggage?"

"At the hotel."

"Are you staying long?"

"For as long as it takes."

It was a strange conversation and quickly going nowhere.

Laila faced Hudson, arms folded tightly across her chest. What she really wanted to do was fling herself at him and tell him just how much she missed him.

She tried again. "Do you have business in town?"

"You could say that."

Hudson looked at her with such intensity and longing she could practically feel the heat coming off his skin.

Her stomach clenched and unclenched as she waited for him to say more.

He closed the space between them in two long strides and linked his arms around her neck.

"I've been a damn fool," he admitted.

She went still on the inside. What was he trying to say?

"It's taken me far too long to realize that you're what matters to me, more than any winery, more than being successful, more than anything in the whole wide world."

"And you came to this conclusion overnight?" Laila asked in a tight little voice that didn't sound like hers.

"No. It was seeing you again, spending time

with you. I didn't think it was possible to miss another human being as much as I miss you."

She'd waited a long time for him to come around. But now she needed a whole lot more than empty words.

"Then why haven't you called me, Hudson?"

"I did. I called you several times, but I kept getting voice mail."

"And you never left a message."

Hudson kissed the top of her head. "Sure I did. You never returned my calls, so I thought I would respect your wishes and leave you alone. Shall we chalk this up to a misunderstanding?"

He was holding her too close, so close she couldn't think.

"It feels so good to hold you and touch you," Hudson whispered in her ear. "I don't ever want to let you go. I love you, Laila."

Laila's insides were Jell-O. Hudson was going soft on her, getting all emotional and mushy.

She wasn't about to be a pushover.

"I want you to give us another shot," he pleaded. "We're good together."

Mariner was still circling and sniffing. Laila was ridiculously happy and sniffing back tears. It seemed she'd waited for an eternity to get here.

"Come on, baby, I know I've been a fool. I didn't think I was worthy of you," Hudson cajoled. "I needed to be successful so that I had something to offer you."

"You are successful. You've always been successful. That's how I always saw you."

Hudson's response was astounding. Who would ever believe that he thought he wasn't good enough for her?

"All I ever wanted was you," Laila said, her eyes brimming with unshed tears. "Not what you owned or what you were worth, just you."

"And you are all that I ever wanted. You inspire me with your unselfish outlook on life. Most women who stood to gain money from royalties would spend it all on themselves, but not you. I'm here to ask you to come back to Washington with me. Help me to earn those royalties for you."

"Hudson, I have a boat, friends, a life."

"Will this help?"

He took a jewelry box from his pocket and snapped it open.

Laila held her breath.

"It's not a ring, at least not yet. It's a charm to add to that broken bracelet, which, by the way, I'm paying to have repaired. The diamond heart's been engraved. Read it."

"'U have my heart,'" Laila gasped, reading out loud. "Oh, Hudson."

Tears spilled down her face as she leaned in to kiss him. When the kiss deepened, Laila ignored both the dog and the banging on her door. It had to be Kent on the other end. She'd missed their sailing date.

She could not deny her feelings. Hudson Godfrey was the only man for her.

She'd always known that, and now he'd come through.